THE SUB

Karen Mercury

MENAGE EVERLASTING

Siren Publishing, Inc.
www.SirenPublishing.com

A SIREN PUBLISHING BOOK
IMPRINT: Ménage Everlasting

THE SUBLIME MISS PAIGE

ISBN: 978-1-62740-413-6

First Printing: August 2013

Cover design by Les Byerley

Printed in the U.S.A.

PUBLISHER
Siren Publishing, Inc.
www.SirenPublishing.com

DEDICATION

To David Grundman
A Menace to The West.

THE SUBLIME MISS PAIGE

KAREN MERCURY

Chapter One

Last Chance, California

This should have been one of the best weeks of Willow Paige's life.

A whole new start in a whole new town. Last Chance was a forgotten burg in the Coachella Valley of California—a place where one could hide, yet close enough to the kitsch and glitz of Palm Springs that she could go there to party, if she ever chose to.

Gentrification was spreading to Last Chance. That's what the realtor—her friend—Jaclyn had assured her. Over in Palm Springs and its environs, flippers were taking advantage of the newfound craze for mid-century modernism, the Jetsons architecture. The clean lines, the abundance of glass, the indoor-outdoor living style perfectly suited Willow's mindset. Or, at least, the mindset she *wished* to have. She wanted a modern vibe, dammit! Willow longed to be supersonic and out of sight. After the humidity of Florida, she wanted the dry, wide-open vistas. The breathtaking views of the craggy San Jacinto Mountains were supposed to give her an expansive feeling, the perfect antidote to the muggy claustrophobia of the Everglades that had been her home for thirty-two years.

The Everglades that had turned into a haunted town of horrors for the past two years.

She had done everything in her power to get as far away from Florida as possible. Purchasing this rundown Searchlight Motel, throwing herself into the renovation. The poolside patio. The breezeways between the wings. The old-time supper club where she sat now, The Cavern on the Green, would be her jewel in the crown.

Now Willow sat in a white plastic Eames chair that was really quite uncomfortable, if stylishly retro. “Dammit, Jaclyn! I’m telling you, you don’t know Matt. At least the Matt that I’ve seen the past two years. You give him too much credit, thinking he’d care.”

Jaclyn sat patiently, her hands folded between her knees. Her real estate business was booming thanks to the alleged end of the economic downturn, but Jaclyn seemed to genuinely enjoy hanging around Willow and helping with the remodel. “I know I’ve never met him. But I feel that I know *you*. And I can’t see *you* marrying an asshole.”

Standing, Willow paced, swinging her arms and breathing deeply. “He changed, Jaclyn. I told you about how he cleaned the kitchen counter after I moved out.”

“Which he’d never once done.”

“Which he’d never once done before, but he did it that once to make sure I’d see the one pristine, perfect photo of the bimbo he was fucking that he set right in the middle of the shiny, clean counter.”

Jaclyn sighed. She was apparently perfectly content with her current asshole, a schlubby but tolerable guy who didn’t even get her a card for her birthday and spent all his time at monster truck rallies. Jaclyn rose from her burnt orange chair. “He was probably just reacting to you leaving him. He was just lashing out. This is a *dog* we’re talking here, Willow. Some men might be assholes about certain subjects, but he’d have to be the lowest of the low to be insensitive about a dog. Matt was her dad, too, right?”

Willow *wanted* to believe Jaclyn was right. She fingered a heavy glass ashtray that would be used for candies. The orange and sea-foam green motif of the supper club was supposed to be comforting, to hearken diners back to simple, reassuring days. She really, really wanted to believe Jaclyn was right, and Matt would at least have sympathy that their beloved Newfoundland dog of eight years had died of lymphoma. Only three weeks after diagnosis and boom, Stormy was gone. Willow had often felt that she loved Stormy more than she loved Matt, especially the past two years. For one, when she thought of Stormy she did not think of betrayal, viciousness, or lies. Dogs were gentle, with not a mean bone in their bodies. Stormy had always been there for her. Suddenly, she was gone.

If Matt couldn't hit the mute button on the Hitler Channel or put down his drugs for *that*, well…it would really be no different than the emotional zombie he'd turned into the past two years. "Okay. I suppose you're right. I should at least give him the benefit of the doubt."

"Yes!" Jaclyn was a good cheerleader. "Willow, he's going to want to know that Stormy passed. No man is *that* cold-hearted."

"Unless the Hitler Channel is on." Willow shouldn't make fun of Jaclyn's Fernando for his monster truck obsession. Matt was just as bad with his nonstop World War II shows, or any show that involved shooting a deer or elk. "He may not care what I do, but he's going to want to know about Stormy."

"Good. I'm glad you made up your mind. Believe you me, you'll feel better once you tell him. If you didn't tell him, you'd be just as bad as him. I know you. You're better than that. Oh, and don't forget about that collector coming by at five thirty."

"*What* collector?"

"Remember? I texted you. That *Three's Company* expert who thinks there might be some collectible owned by Norman Fell around here somewhere."

Willow was aghast. "*Norman Fell?* Isn't he that guy who played the roommates' super on *Three's Company?*" The concept that there even *was* such a thing as a *Three's Company* expert was almost funny enough to take Willow's mind off her dog and her asinine ex-husband. There was a celebrity-obsessed culture in the nearby Palm Springs area, so it shouldn't surprise her.

"That's the guy. Mr. Roper. Well, you know that in its fifties incarnation as the Sunset Palomino Ranch, this place was a well-known swinging bordello. Maybe Norman had some sojourns here and this expert wants to profit off the memorabilia."

Willow scoffed. "Like what? A bottle of Norman's motion lotion? Oh, whatever. The guy can look around all he wants as long as one of us is with him."

"Well, don't take too long showing him Mr. Fell's smut collection," said Jaclyn, standing at the swinging glass door. "We're meeting Fernando and his friend at Sprockets at six-thirty."

"Oh, jeez," whined Willow. She hadn't particularly wanted to meet Fernando's monster truck friend, but she knew that she "should" move on with her life. It had been four months since she had made the final break with Matt. Then she had had to deal with Stormy's cancer, not to mention the myriad tasks and chores that came with renovating a motel. She felt she was probably going to have a heart attack from stress if she didn't kick back, have a couple drinks, and allow some man to buy her dinner, even if he did talk about scaled-up dune buggies the whole time.

"He's cute, I guarantee you."

"Yeah, yeah. I'm sure he's cute. See you at Sprockets." Willow waved. She knew Fernando. She had seen Jaclyn's idea of "cute." Not all men could or should be carved pieces of man candy, and it wasn't any man's fault he had a bald gene. But he could avoid the Bozo look by getting a trim around the shirt collar—and clipping the nose and ear hair wouldn't be amiss, either. Willow just didn't know how Jaclyn could sleep with Fernando.

But Willow was starting to wonder if she could sleep with *any* man, however. She had dated Matt for four years then had two years of relative happiness in marriage before everything fell apart. All told, it had been eight years since she had kissed another man. Just the thought of doing so creeped her out.

To get out of earshot of some workers who were hammering, Willow moved out by the pool that was fringed by palms. Her heart sped up at the thought of calling Matt. She had struggled on many occasions to refrain from calling him. She knew it wasn't a good idea in general. This Matt wasn't the man she had married. He had changed irrevocably. Yet why did she still long for him so badly?

She knew it was human nature to want to be loved, to be cherished, nurtured, and treated well. Matt was the most recent, or only, man who had done that. It was just natural to long for his kind tone of voice, to hear him call her "pussy willow," to hear the dreaded "L word."

He probably won't answer anyway. He's been screening my calls for months. Years. Oh, hell. I'll just act casual, emotionless, and insensitive...like he's done to me the past two years.

"Hi, Matt."

"Willow!" Matt was obviously surprised to hear her voice. *No doubt he's expecting one of his other bimbos.* Already he was making getting-off-the-phone sounds. "Ah, I have to—"

Willow cut him off. "It's okay, Matt. I won't keep you long. I just thought you might want to know. Three weeks ago Stormy was diagnosed with lymphoma."

For once, Matt was silent.

It occurred to Willow why he was so stupefied. "That's a type of cancer."

"Oh."

He must be in shock. Of course. That's understandable. "Anyway, they gave her two months to live. But she took a turn for the worse after three weeks."

"Oh."

"I had to send her to the Rainbow Bridge at the vet's office. It was my only option, Matt. It would've been cruel to keep her lingering any longer."

"Oh. Well, yeah. That would be cruel. Wow, that's sad to hear. Say, can I call you back? I'm just saying goodbye to a guest. I'll call you back in ten minutes."

What? It was Willow's turn to be stunned into silence. How important could *any* guest be compared to the death of a beloved pet? She had prepared to steel herself against Matt's insensitivity, but this even took *that* coldhearted cake. "What?" she breathed. "Matt, you're just incredible! Can't whoever is trying to leave just hang tight for thirty seconds? Is he some damned bank president or something? Even bank presidents might understand that your dog passed away!"

Matt began to stammer. "Oh, hey, before you go. Can you remind me which company we used for our homeowners insurance? I can't fucking find anything around here. There's mold on the bathroom ceiling and—"

Willow punched the *end call* button so hard she nearly broke her thumb. Then she flung the phone into the pool.

Of course, she immediately knew her error and had to look for the long-handled net to fish it out. *Damn! This is supposed to be my great, new life! Then why is everything so utterly screwed?* She was so emotional she didn't know whether to scream or cry. While she was patting her cell dry she bashed the toe of her flat shoe against some kind of stupid plastic bucket full of cement, and she howled like one of the coyotes she often heard in the desert at night.

The howl was a mixture of anguish and rage, and it rolled piercingly down the breezeway between two motel room wings. Several contractors who were surfacing the swimming pool froze and looked at her curiously, but Willow kept it up because it felt good. She wasn't sure whether she would burst into tears or scream in anger at her soon-to-be-ex-husband. She stood with arms out stiffly at her sides, looking into the sky like an ape-man who had just discovered fire.

"*Fucktard!*" was the first discernible word that came from her lungs. As a few cement masons laughed at her, she sprung into action, heading down the breezeway toward the front lobby where her office was. "*Fucking fucktard! Epic assmunching asshat!*" It felt good to swear. She thought she recalled a news article that said swearing helped ease pain. "Fucking coke-snorting dickwad!"

Jamming her butt into the chair, Willow rolled into a decrepit turquoise filing cabinet that had been there when she'd taken possession of the Searchlight Motel. She had shoved some important papers in here—maybe Matt's stupid insurance papers were there. She would dearly love to hire a motel manager, but with only thirty rooms, she really couldn't justify that. Besides, she had been a secretary before and during her marriage to Matt. If she couldn't organize some damned papers…

What's this? Willow's anger at her dickhead ex-spouse went completely out the window when her fingers touched a worn, glossy piece of folded black cardboard that declared it was a menu. That would definitely be a great discovery to find an old menu for the Cavern on the Green.

However, the menu was for the "World Famous Sunset Palomino Ranch Bordello." It must be from the fifties when the Searchlight was a bordello. They even had a tagline, "Not Just Sex—A Trip!" This was a potentially even better find. A bordello had a menu? This would be the epitome of kitsch. She could frame it for the lobby. Willow's heart raced as she opened up the folded cardboard.

The Best Fillies in California!
Ranch Delights

Holy shit! There were menu items such as a Salt and Pepper Party, a 69 Party, a Pony Express, and a Filly Steak Sandwich. A fellow could, apparently, order a Trojan Horse, a Horse and Buggy, or have an Irish Cream Party conjured up for him.

Willow's mind reeled, wondering at the meaning behind some of the menu items. A Feast at the Y seemed pretty straightforward. But what in the hell was a Sex on the Beach—doing it in a sandbox? And didn't pretty much every man want a Low-Fat Delight? Of course, only if he wanted to avoid a Cream Pie or, God forbid, a Milky Way.

Reading the sultry and forbidden names made Willow's heart slow, and a warmth spread between her thighs. It had been a very long time since she'd been toyed with anything close to lust or passion. She knew the hookers behind this menu weren't in the passion business, but a little lust around now wouldn't go amiss in Willow's new world. Of course, it would be ideal if there were actual feelings behind it. That was probably too much to ask. Willow thought she might be ready for plain old lust again soon.

She didn't have much experience with men. After all, she was only thirty-two and had wasted eight years on Matt. Her most arousing memory had been during a college break in Daytona Beach. She had witnessed two men doing unnatural, erotic things to each other in an alley. But boy, had she longed to join in. *Great. My most sensual experience, and I was just a spectator.*

She was excited by the activities suggested in the menu but also afraid of them.

Willow wasn't even aware that her jaw was hanging open until a figure appeared in the office doorway. She looked up stupidly, making a noise that approximated "eh?"

The silhouette was delicious enough to take Willow's mind off the menu for a few seconds. He was tall and lean, a "long, cool drink of water" as they said in the west. A drip of sweat rolled down between her breasts. This was one thing she already disliked about the Coachella Valley. She wasn't slender enough to wear the fashions that the hundred degree June weather required, so she felt very self-conscious in sleeveless, low-cut shirts. She wore them nevertheless, because the air conditioning wasn't functioning yet. And this man's level, assessing gaze made her feel highly self-conscious. It was as though he had X-ray vision and could see her thunder thighs through her flippy miniskirt.

When he stepped into the office away from the backlit doorway, she could see he was a stunning man, with the chiseled features of a Marlboro stud. His closely-shaven auburn hair looked soft like a brush. Although he wore a button-down jean material shirt with the sleeves rolled up to the elbows like some sort of professional, she could tell in an instant he was built, cut and carved like a turkey. "Mrs. Paige," the man assumed, with a bit of a drawl. He almost sounded Irish.

"*Miss* Willow Paige," she corrected him.

He reached out a hand for her to shake. "Steffen Jung."

It occurred to her. *This is the guy Jaclyn warned me about.* The Norman Fell fan who was looking for smut magazines. *This might be the artifact he's looking for.* Willow dropped the menu back into the file drawer and slammed it shut. She wasn't about to sell the menu. She shuddered to think the menu had anything to do with Norman Fell.

Smiling artificially, she stood and shook his manly hand with her clammy one. "Yes. You're the guy looking for some *Three's Company* memorabilia."

He frowned. "*Three's Company?* That show with John Ritter?"

Willow was less self-assured now. "The show with Norman Fell?" It was more a question than a statement.

Steffen grinned seductively. "Well, Norman Fell was a member of Frank Sinatra's Rat Pack. That would explain why someone would be here looking for some memorabilia of his."

"You're kidding me. The super on *Three's Company* was a Rat Packer? Well, if I would've known that, I would've named a suite after him. Which artifact exactly are you looking for? I'll let you know if I've come across it."

"Well, as much as I'd like to find Mrs. Roper's housecoat, I'm actually here to sign off on your building renovation."

"Ah, excuse me? Sign off on what, exactly?"

"Oh." Steffen took a business card from his front shirt pocket and handed it to Willow.

The card was steamy, having been against his chest. Automatically, Willow's pussy shivered with delight, and she imagined she could smell his musky sweat emanating from the damp card.

Steffen Jung
Chief Building Inspector
City of Palm Springs

Oh, dear. He was here to inspect her plumbing, not ask for a Cream Pie.

Chapter Two

Steffen was amused by the beautiful woman's cluelessness. He *was* carrying a clipboard and had about a hundred keys jangling from a belt loop of his 501 jeans. He thought it was pretty obvious that he was a building inspector and not a memorabilia collector. Steffen was very familiar with those celebrity vultures who crawled all over construction sites, looking for schmaltzy items from the fifties or sixties when Palm Springs was in its heyday. Steffen himself had an intense interest in preserving mid-century architecture and loved to help owners get the remodeling details just right for the era. He hated those celebrity vultures with a passion. They were only in it for the bucks. Whenever Steffen stumbled across an artifact, he either made sure the owner preserved it or gave it to a museum.

He said, "I just want to see how you're coming on your improvements." He looked at his checklist. "HVAC, the swimming pool, plumbing. Looks like the last guy out here never signed off on your Phase I electrical. Let's start with the circuit panel, make sure it's properly grounded out and won't electrocute anyone."

"Circuit panel? Uh, I think I know where that is. I think it's actually in a storage area next to the Cesar Romero Room." Miss Paige turned and looked down at a vintage turquoise filing cabinet as though maybe it contained the key to the Cesar Romero Room. From this angle Steffen could appreciate the slope of her shapely ass. Her hips flared beautifully from her waistline, and her clingy short skirt swayed when she moved.

He chuckled. "The Cesar Romero Room? I'd like to see some recent plans for this building too. I could help you naming some rooms, for example. I *am* sort of an aficionado of mid-century modernist buildings. The Coachella Valley has the highest concentration of them in the world. I'm on the executive board of the Palm Springs Modern Committee. You might want to join, too, seeing as you've got an obvious interest in preserving that era."

She turned back to him, chipper now, having apparently decided not to open the file cabinet. She, too, had a belt slung low on her lovely hips, with almost the same amount of keys as Steffen had. She fingered them as she led the way back into the breezeway. "That *does* sound intriguing, Mr. Jung. I haven't been here long—I just chose Last Chance, really, because it was cheaper than Palm Springs proper. I lived in Florida near Gainesville my entire life until recently. When I saw this rundown motel I just knew I had to have it. This area has a lot of similarities to Florida, actually."

Steffen peeked into a few rooms that were somewhat furnished. He saw pieces by Eames—or Eames knockoffs at least—Lasky and McCobb. White globe pendant lamps, burnt orange pop-art fabric, metal wall sculptures, and the clean lines of Scandinavian wood were highly featured. He thought he spied a Steve Reiner original chaise longue in one room. "You've done a good job. Do you have a David Niven Room?"

Turning, she looked at him curiously. "You're kidding me. Don't tell me David Niven was a Rat Packer. I guess you really *could* tell me a lot about this era. I do have a Swifty Lazar Room," she said proudly.

"Actually, Sinatra hated the term 'Rat Pack.' He called it 'that stupid phrase.'"

Steffen immediately regretted that he had crushed the girl. She stopped walking. Her open, trusting face wrinkled in disappointment, framed so prettily by long ash-blonde hair. "Well. I suppose I'll have to change the name of my Rat Pack Suite."

Steffen said cheerily, "I saw you have a pétanque court." Pétanque was a game like bocce ball gaining popularity in the valley. Willow's lovely new gravel court was on a knoll by a pristine lawn with an expansive view of the San Jacinto Mountains. Steffen could see she had a flair for hotel management. Seeing the court and lawn made him immediately want to sit at the poolside bar and order a Bellini or gimlet.

His ruse worked. Willow continued walking and said happily, “Yes, I’m going to sling some hammocks out there between palm trees. You don’t sound American. How’d you come to like this style of architecture?”

“I was born in Heidelberg but raised in County Kerry, Ireland.”

Willow paused, about to fit the key into the utility room door. She seemed so entranced with Steffen’s background her fingers just hovered near the keyhole. “Ah. Army brat?”

“Yes. We moved to Palm Springs when I was in high school.” Steffen’s dad was an army engineer who had praised him, given him the confidence to succeed—the self-assurance required to bed hundreds of women. Suddenly, though, just meeting Willow Paige made him take a different tack. He needed to step more gently with her. He couldn’t just toy with her. She wasn’t that easy.

“I see. That’s why I couldn’t pinpoint your accent.” She looked so long at him she seemed to have forgotten about the key. Her eyes grew soft and moist and she seemed fixated by his mouth, a feature he’d always hated. He thought his mouth was grim, his lips too thin, so he tried to compensate by smiling a lot.

He pointed at a nearby closed door. “The Cesar Romero Room.”

She blinked. “Yes! How’d you know that?”

“The plaque on the door was a giveaway,” he suggested.

Once inside the utility room, Steffen inspected the circuit panel. Everything looked properly grounded out. Next he wanted to check if the completed plumbing was up to code, look at venting ducts in the kitchen, and check the automatic sprinkler system. An inspector beneath Steffen had signed off on the Phase I framing and sheetrock, but Steffen wanted to see the final phases of this retro beauty himself.

"This is weird," said Willow in a faraway voice.

Steffen chuckled, scribbling on a form on his clipboard. "That's not a phrase that a permit applicant usually uses around an inspector." But when he looked up, it was his turn to gasp in surprise.

Willow stood with hands on hips, examining the contraption. "What *is* it?"

Steffen knew exactly what it was. He had game, for better or worse. He knew the ins and outs. If he hadn't seen it all as an inspector, he had personal experience with St. Andrew's Crosses. Black, padded two-by-fours were crossed and bolted to header beams at a height of about seven feet. The builder had rendered it moveable by attaching it to a supporting frame with wheels. The footrest would render it more stable, Steffen could see. The builder had smartly bolted suspension cuffs at a reasonable height so that even a short woman wouldn't suffer unduly when strapped in.

"Hm," said Steffen, examining the cuffs with a professional air. "Fleece lined. Looks like real fleece, too."

Willow frowned at him. "What *is* it? I promise you, Mr. Inspector, I've never seen this thing before in my life, and I've been inside this utility room, obviously."

Steffen watched her face carefully for a reaction. "It's a bondage cross." Understanding slowly spread over her face. "See these cuffs? Because of the angle of the cross, the submissive wouldn't actually have to *dangle*, but the builder went through the trouble of using suspension cuffs which reduce the chance for injury. See? Her feet would actually rest on this foot board—"

"I *see!*" Willow backed away with arms crossed in front of her abdomen in a protective stance. Her eyes flashed with shock, as though Steffen had built the contraption himself. "I promise you I have no idea what it's doing in my establishment! It wasn't here before!"

Steffen held his hands up in a calming gesture. “Miss, miss. It’s all right. I’m not going to cite you for it. It’s hardly against the law between consensual adults.”

She was calmer now. “I know. I just didn’t want you to think that *I*...condoned or planned...This is not *that sort* of establishment!”

Steffen chuckled. “I didn’t think it was, Miss Paige! It’s obviously a leftover attraction from this place’s glory days as a bordello. It’s actually an exciting find, I think.”

Willow seemed to even warm to the odd structure now. She smiled a little as she examined it from all angles. With a wicked glint in her eye, she asked, “And how do you know it’s a ‘her’ who would be attached to this cross? Hm? Why not a ‘he’?”

She was a strange one! First protesting that she was not a regular user of the St. Andrew’s Cross—as though he would assume she had brought it with her from Florida to store in a utility room—and now making slyly erotic insinuations! Steffen casually gripped the padded header bar with one hand and looked down at the little minx. It must be over a hundred in the stifling utility room with no AC, and a rivulet of sweat dampened her yellow T-shirt between her breasts. Her bra must have been soaked because the outline of her nipples clearly stood out. He shouldn’t be noticing these things about a permit applicant in a work environment. But it was hard to ignore her voluptuous form, her sublime, almost angelic face. “Indeed, Miss Paige.”

She became even bolder. “Call me Willow.”

“Willow. Indeed, why not a fellow? See, a submissive could be faced either way. Toward the cross, or with *his* back to the cross. Each position has different pros and cons.”

Her intrigue was plain. “I don’t want you to think I’m a complete prude.”

“The people who protest that they’re not prudish are usually the ones who are. It’s all right. It’s nothing to be ashamed of. I know today's modern world puts pressure on people to be so-called 'open-minded.' Lots of people just aren't cut from that cloth."

She stuck out a stubborn lower lip. She had to look at his clavicle to make her next confession. "I may have just wasted eight years with a, uh, an *unimaginative* dull man—"

"Vanilla."

As expected, she looked confused. "Yes, boring and flavored like vanilla. But don't think I'm inexperienced. I had an experience in Daytona Beach I'll never forget. Things get pretty crazy there during spring break, believe you me."

"Oh, yeah?" Why did she care what he thought? That was an encouraging sign. A woman with no interest in him wouldn't give a shit what he thought. "What happened in Daytona Beach?"

Willow looked from side to side as though someone was eavesdropping, and she lowered her voice. She even gripped the St. Andrew's Cross, too. "Well. I was coming out of a nightclub around midnight, you know, through the side door that leads into an alley. Of course I was with two girlfriends, I'd never go clubbing that late alone, but they were so drunk they were sort of stumbling ahead of me. I noticed two men behind a parked car. One was leaning against the wall, but the other was down on his knees and—"

"All *right!*" It sounded as though Gomer Pyle had just stepped into the utility room. Even the fellow's silhouette made him look like Bart Simpson's bus driver. His spindly arms stuck out from an oversize T-shirt, and his long dark hair was like an unkempt pyramid. "Ronnie Dobbs here, at your service. Is this the place I come to appraise Norman Fell's watch? Hoo-wee! It's hotter than a two-peckered billy goat in here! Oh Lord, did I interrupt something? Someone said a Miss Willow Paige was down here? Wow-wee, that sure is some well-made bondage cross. Ha-ha! Well, lookie here, a Betty Boop love meter!"

Instinctively, Steffen stepped between Willow and the intruder. The fellow had round, bulging cartoon eyes, and he wore long shorts that would have been at home on a Lil' Rascal. "Listen here. Miss Paige is in a meeting. Why don't you just march back down the hall to her office and wait for her there?"

The goofball cringed back in mock fear. "Well, well! I'd say you're more of a too-hot-to-handle lover boy than a Frigidaire!"

What was this idiotic appraiser going on about? Having been raised around military men, Steffen knew the value of manners. But having been raised around military men, he also knew the value of a well-placed fist. "Listen here, you half-witted twat—"

Willow insinuated herself between the men. "I think he's talking about that Betty Boop love meter over there, Steffen."

Steffen blinked and looked. Willow was right. A vintage slot machine against the wall depicted Betty Boop asking, "Hot how are you?" Apparently one of ten answers was "lover boy."

Ronnie Dobbs wiped his brow. "I didn't mean no harm. It's hotter than a pair of sweatpants full of barbecue, Lord. Sometimes I just can't help insulting people. I had a very rough childhood, so people usually let me get away with it. I think that's why I like to collect old-timey toys and suchlike. It just brings me back to a more innocent time, you know, buddy?"

"I suppose," Steffen said grudgingly. He knew that was why he was an aficionado of mid-century architecture. It symbolized more innocent times, when people did healthy, wholesome things and were way more easily amused.

But Ronnie Dobbs just had to continue on. "Times when people played with Transformers, back when you could be satisfied with a good ole bottle of Night Train or Thunderbird, you know? Back when your old lady couldn't have you arrested just by pointing a finger at you and saying 'Officer, I swear he just bashed me in the head with that six-pack of Old Milwaukee.' Shee, I haven't drank an Old Milwaukee in three years, how would that bitch know—"

Steffen finally exploded. "All right, that's it!" Grabbing Mr. Dobbs by the front of his shirt, he gave him the bum's rush out the door of the utility room. He didn't set him loose in the hallway, either, but continued hustling him down the hallway. Ronnie half-walked and half-flew by the seat of his pants. "We've heard enough, you twisted bugger! Miss Paige doesn't want to sell you any damned wristwatch. I don't want to see you hanging around here anymore, hear me? And I'm gonna be around here plenty, keeping an eye out."

"You can't do this to me!" Ronnie Dobbs wailed as he was ejected toward the parking lot. Steffen wanted to follow, to see what kind of vehicle he got into and make note of his license plate number. "I'm an honest memorabilia collector looking for artifacts! I ain't a sleazebag like those douchefaces who try and make money off other people's sorrows!"

Steffen jammed his hands onto his hips. "Oh, yeah? Then why do you want Norman Fell's watch?"

"I *keep* it! I *collect* them! I'm the keeper of the collectibles, like!"

"Well, it's not going to do anyone any good sitting in your closet now, is it?" Steffen pointed with a stiff arm. "Get out of here, you dirtbag! There are plenty of workers in there with heavy equipment I could order down on your head, so *get!*"

Ronnie Dobbs finally climbed behind the wheel of an old, battered pickup. He tried to burn rubber out of the lot but only succeeded in stalling the engine. While restarting it, he shrieked out the window, "You'll be sorry! I'm not the 'most arrested man in the Coachella Valley' for nothing!"

"Is that so?" Steffen mused quietly. "I'll thank him for informing us of that."

Willow exhaled loudly when Mr. Dobbs finally drove off. Steffen turned to her. He'd been so keyed up getting rid of the repulsive collector he hadn't thought how this altercation might have affected her. Now he just wanted to put his arms around her and soothe her, though of course that would be ridiculous. They barely knew each other and had a professional relationship.

"Jeez, that was strange," breathed Willow, her hand on her stomach.

"I'm sorry about that. I hope you didn't have a sweet deal going with Mr. Dobbs there that I just ruined. But that guy was over the top. He was out of control."

"Oh, I couldn't agree more! Come, what's next on your list?"

Steffen looked at his clipboard. "Ah, vents in the kitchen." They started walking. "Listen. Who's your foreman? I need to talk to him anyway about a couple of items I see aren't finished. But I want to warn him about that Dobbs character. He seems overly obsessed with this alleged watch. Have you actually *found* any watch?"

"My foreman is Chas White, but he's usually difficult to find. No, I haven't even found any damned watch, that's the strange part. My realtor just an hour ago told me to expect this guy. She didn't describe which artifact he wanted. I've found several, as you can imagine."

"Well, find out where she found that crackpot. I don't want him around you."

Willow looked at him from underneath her eyelashes. "That's very sweet of you." They had obviously already stepped beyond the boundaries of an inspector-permittee relationship, and Steffen wished intensely he could step even farther. He had the feeling, though, that Willow had to allow him. She would give him the sign. "What I want to know is, how did that damned bondage cross get into my utility room? And Ronnie Dobbs seemed to instantly know what it was."

Steffen didn't point out that he had also instantly known what it was, too. Willow was the only one who hadn't. Steffen thought it was sort of cute that she wasn't jaded like so many Southern Californians. Maybe she thought the St. Andrew's Cross was a football tackling dummy. "I have a suspicion about that," Steffen said. "There's a connecting door from the Cesar Romero Room next door to the utility room. How much remodeling have you done in Cesar's room?"

"Oh, that one has barely been touched. The door is a bitch to get open and I need one of these carpenters to take a look at it. See?"

Steffen tried the knob. It didn't turn at all, but there was a two-inch crack through which he could see stacked boxed and other large, darkened objects. "The door could be warped and need to be planed," Steffen suggested. He was going to suggest they try the adjoining door from the utility room—he didn't usually like to butt into rooms that weren't on his inspection sheet—but the curiosity, and his interest in Miss Paige, were overwhelming. However, his cell phone buzzed. His dispatcher had texted, "Mr. Barbieri at Lone Palm wants to know if you can come now instead of at six."

He told Willow, "Apparently my next appointment was just moved up. I'd like to come back tomorrow if that's all right. Check the kitchen, plumbing, see the progress on the HVAC." Actually, he just wanted to come back, period.

"Sure." Was it his imagination she seemed more excited than most permit applicants? "Maybe by that time, I'll have this door open. This is a big, exciting mystery!"

"If there's a watch in there, don't tell that whack-a-mole," Steffen suggested. "And I'd like to finish hearing the end of your story."

"Story?"

"You were telling me about something that happened in Daytona Beach ten years ago. You saw two men in an alley."

"Oh." She visibly reddened, and started walking toward the pétanque court, toward the lawn, away from the workers. "Yes. Daytona Beach. I guess I just didn't want you thinking I was some kind of prudish schoolmarm."

"You can tell me," Steffen encouraged. "Believe you me, I see *all* sorts of odd things in this business."

They both faced the same way, standing on the lawn looking out at the vast bowl of desert ranch land and gypsum mines. "Well, I wouldn't call it 'odd' per se. I was very excited and interested." She scooted closer to Steffen so she could speak more quietly. "Like I said, one man leaned back against the wall, another man on his knees before him. He was obviously…"

"Giving him a blow job." Steffen filled in.

"Yes. I must've been a bit drunk myself, because I stumbled *toward* them, away from my friends, and just stood there like a slack-jawed moron."

"But you liked what you saw."

"Yes. They were very young and buff and...hungry. They didn't seem to care who saw them coupling like that in an alleyway. The one receiving the..."

"Blow job."

"Blow job, he looked me right in the eyes. I mean, I'm sure they were gay, and that I was watching didn't turn them on in the slightest."

"Or maybe they were exhibitionists."

"Oh, yes." Willow's ardor practically simmered, like heat waves emanating from her body. "But he locked eyes with me and didn't look away, not even while he was choking and gasping and..."

"Coming."

"Yes, coming." Suddenly Willow inhaled and exhaled loudly, and finally turned to Steffen. "Whew! I don't know what prompted *that* memory! Well, the St. Andrew's Cross, obviously." She stuck out a hand for Steffen to shake, as though they had just discussed her roofing.

Steffen was so aroused as he shook her hand, he knew his erection would be evident, cradled in his 501s. That cut of jeans didn't leave much to the imagination, so he swiftly turned away from the valley, back toward the parking lot. "I've got to get over to Lone Palm Ranch. Guy's added a tack room. He's your neighbor, actually. You can see the cattle from here."

"Oh, I used to love riding horses in Florida. I could do that, if I could ever get an hour away from this damned remodel. Well, I've got a dinner to go to. I suppose that'll be my public outing for the month."

Willow's rueful sigh led Steffen to believe she wasn't that excited about the prospect of the dinner date. As he walked back to his company truck, he realized he was jealous of her date. Just as fervently as he wanted to keep Ronnie Dobbs off the property of the Searchlight Motel, he wanted to know which knuckle-dragger was taking Willow to dinner.

All the way down into the valley, Steffen couldn't stop thinking about the shapely motel owner. She was quite a gem, just like her lovely Desert Modern establishment. Yes. She was sublime, and he simply had to have her.

Chapter Three

"Okay, I'm going to have to issue a stop work order," said Steffen Jung. He stood on nearly the top step of an eight foot ladder looking at the ceiling of the new tack room. His well-rounded ass in the tight, worn jeans was so luscious Amadeo's penis lengthened and plumped. Just watching this delicious specimen of manhood stand, move—hell, do *anything*— was a joy to behold. "The structural plans for ceiling joists were approved using two-by-fours. Your contractor used one-by-fours. And this load-bearing beam is only a double two-by-ten. Should be a triple."

"Uh-huh," Amadeo said vaguely, practically drooling as he looked up. Steffen Jung had aged like a fine wine in the twenty-two years—*Jesus, has it been that long? I feel ancient*—since high school. It was obvious Steffen didn't remember Amadeo, who had been a sophomore when Steffen had reigned as varsity quarterback, homecoming king, and masturbation fantasy for every horny teenage girl, and young men of certain inclinations. Such as Amadeo.

"And these metal gussets are much too feeble. Where'd he get them, a cereal box?"

"Uh-huh." Amadeo was practically senseless with lust. Usually boys who were hotshots in school turned out to be doughy bastards and losers later in life. That had been his experience, anyway. He ran into some of those high school jocks in his forays into Last Chance or Palm Springs for supplies. He'd even stumbled into a few of them at the Racquet Club, the coed bondage dungeon in Last Chance. He'd had the unfortunate experience of viewing a member of the high school wrestling team in one room at the club, swinging spread-legged trussed up in a sling. That image had ruined any play for the entire night—and for many nights thereafter. Latex G-strings would just never be the same again.

But Steffen Jung was finer than ever. He had even improved with age, if such a thing was possible. He had grown into his looks. The slight crow's feet at the corners of his eyes, the stubble sprinkled across his chiseled jaw, the sinewy forearms when he made a fist and knocked on a beam—Amadeo was entranced. Whereas the other jocks seemed to have slid into a careless mindset where they let their bodies go, maybe thinking that after age thirty it was all downhill, the forty-year-old Steffen was more superb than ever, more carved than any of the vaqueros or hands who worked for Amadeo.

"Who's your contractor, anyway?"

When Steffen looked down, Amadeo knew his hard-on was obvious. He wore the leather chaps he favored when he had to ride through the creosote bushes, prickly pear, and ocotillo. They cradled the bulge of his cock nicely. He didn't care. He couldn't care. Steffen obviously didn't recall him from school, and he'd already said he was issuing a stop work order. What did Amadeo have to lose?

"El Mirador Construction. Run by Chas White. Do you know them?"

"Sounds familiar for some reason." Steffen had started to descend the ladder, but stopped, looking into the distance thoughtfully. "Right. The place I was just inspecting, Chas White was the contractor, too. Is he around right now?"

"I doubt it," said Amadeo. "I've never actually seen the guy. That's probably why the workers didn't build it to specs. There seems to be a disconnect between Chas and his men." It was all Amadeo could do to refrain from gripping Steffen by the hips, yanking up his sweaty button-down shirt, and taking an enormous fat lick from his salty abdomen. His face was just two feet from Steffen's glorious crotch, and that was not a gun in the quarterback's pocket, nor was he happy to see Amadeo. No, his dick was long and fat, just as Amadeo recalled it from watching Steffen shower ages ago.

Steffen continued down the ladder, wiping his sawdusty hands on his jeans. "Are there any workers around at the moment, maybe working elsewhere on the property?"

There were some laborers working on the back deck of his house, but Amadeo didn't want to leave the privacy of the tack room. "Where did you just come from? I mean, where else was Chas White working? If his work is shoddy all over town, something should be done."

His ruse worked. Steffen wandered over to a wall where hooks held bits and bridles. Steffen first looked at a regular saddle rack, but his eyes soon wandered to a hook where Amadeo had carelessly slung a few collars, shackles, and cuffs—items obviously too small for horses. One never knew when a playmate would arrive at his ranch. Amadeo did not do long-term relationships, and he didn't associate with his play partners outside of a scene, so he would not be horseback riding with them. But he had already foreseen the endless possibilities when he'd had this new tack room built.

"Oh, it's the new Searchlight Motel that's being refurbished. You know where that is?"

Amadeo came closer to his old idol. "Yeah, I noticed some work being done there." Of course he had. The Searchlight was only about four blocks away from the Racquet Club. "That thing's been decrepit as long as I can remember."

Yes. Steffen was definitely inspecting a studded collar that hung by a D-ring. There could only be one possible use for *that*. "You've been around Last Chance for awhile."

Perhaps it wouldn't be useful to reminisce about the ole Twelve Palms High days until later. Much, much later. Steffen had probably never taken note of Amadeo even back in the day. Amadeo was Italian and had been pretty much a pot-smoking thug, into playing guitar with his grunge band. They definitely had not run with the same crowds. "Yeah. My dad started this ranch when he came here from Italy. I've been stuck here for quite awhile."

"Oh, it's not that bad. I've come to be really fascinated by the architecture." Steffen's tone changed now, and he reached out to finger a pair of fleece-lined handcuffs dangling from a hook. "Hm. This must be the day for finding stuff like this."

What the fuck. Be bold. Go for the gusto. "Stuff like what? Bondage handcuffs?" Amadeo held his breath. The building inspector would either encourage him in his kink or buckle a cuff around his wrist in anger.

Or neither. Steffen finally turned to Amadeo, and his eyes twinkled. "Yeah. Over at the Searchlight, you wouldn't believe what we found. A vintage St. Andrew's Cross."

Amadeo was surprised that the square inspector knew what a St. Andrew's Cross was. "You're kidding," he said warmly. "So it was from the fifties when that place was last operating?"

"Sixties, I imagine. The last revenues from the Searchlight were sixty-five, when everything started going down the tubes in Palm Springs."

"Before the rehab," Amadeo said, actually becoming excited about the subject. "It's just been in the past couple of years I've seen Last Chance coming around again. It was real depressing before that, practically a ghost town." The Racquet Club had opened two years ago to booming business. Other thriving businesses had followed. It only made sense someone would want to remodel the Searchlight.

"Right. These projects are what make being a building inspector worthwhile."

"You mean the Searchlight, not my dull-ass tack room."

"Well, yeah." Was it Amadeo's imagination that Steffen's look actually became sly and almost flirtatious then? Steffen *did* glance back at the cuffs, meaningfully. "But it looks as though you've got a lot in common with the former owners of the Searchlight."

Be bold. Amadeo was accustomed to being bold. "You mean collect bondage artifacts? I don't just *collect* them. Most of mine have gotten a bit of use. This particular pair"—and he swiped the cuffs from the hook to fondle them admiringly—"just happens to be new. You never know when you might have a sudden need for a good set of cuffs. Was the cross in good shape?"

"Yes. Damned good shape, like barely used. It looked homemade."

"Most of them are, or were, especially back then. You couldn't just walk down to Walmart and pick one up. Could you tell if the owner has any interest in selling?"

"Well, our investigation was sort of cut short—by my appointment with *you*, matter of fact. But yes, I don't think she has any particular interest in keeping the cross. I could ask her. I plan to see her tomorrow. We have a feeling there might be more artifacts hidden around there, but we'll know more tomorrow."

"I'd really appreciate that." Taking another leap of faith, Amadeo plunged ahead. "Fact, we could use a new cross over at the club. Those things get pretty bashed-up with the heavy use they get, and one of ours is about to bite the dust."

"The club?"

"The Racquet Club on Manilow Avenue, just down from the Searchlight."

Amadeo had been in the lifestyle long enough to know the startled look of recognition in someone's face. He wondered if Steffen would admit having been there before. "Oh, sure, the club. Yeah, I think I know the cross you mean. In that room with all of the mirrors, right?"

"Right. Were you at the club to inspect the room addition?"

Steffen grinned so seductively there was no mistaking his attendance at the dungeon. "Nope. No inspection at all, unless you count inspecting the Domme's techniques."

It was impossible to tell if Steffen said “Domme” or “Dom.” But since Amadeo was accustomed to grabbing the bull by the horns, that’s what he did.

Still grinning, Steffen attempted to walk on by Amadeo, out the tack room’s door. Shooting out a hand, Amadeo grabbed the inspector’s forearm and firmly slammed him against a spot on the wall that had been purposefully left bare, aside from a couple of bucket hooks that held no buckets. Steffen was probably so surprised he allowed himself to be slammed, and Amadeo was so experienced within the flashing of an eye he had the building inspector cuffed to a hook, behind his back at waist level.

He only cuffed one wrist, but Steffen didn’t raise a finger to prevent Amadeo from running his face up the sweaty side of Steffen’s throat. It was better than any erotic fantasy, breathing in the salty dampness, the slick moisture against the tip of his nose, the brushing of his lips against the stubbled jaw. It seemed that Steffen even rolled his skull back against the wooden boards to bare his naked throat to Amadeo’s mouth.

“You’re a hot, delicious stud,” Amadeo whispered, taking a slight nip from Steffen’s earlobe. He pinned the other man to the wall with the strength of his hips, making one, two, three immense lunges to massage his stiff cock against Steffen’s crotch. Amadeo was taller than most men—a strapping, six-foot-five Paleolithic hunk of man—but Steffen was substantial enough not to get lost beneath Amadeo’s bulk. When Amadeo swayed his hips into the other man, he felt the rigid bulk of a hard shaft pressing back against him, and he humped even more energetically. The other man’s penis thanked him by nearly bringing him off when he ground against it. The quarterback could not deny that he was turned on. His enormous pulsating schlong was testimony enough.

What a colossal toolbag I am, making a grab for Steffen Jung. But I have nothing to lose. Steffen Jung was already issuing a stop work order. It wasn't Amadeo's fault anyway, about the joists. It was Chas White's fault. Chas White seemed to be a guy they both hated.

Amadeo parted his lips and took some hungry bites from the steamy throat. "How can anyone keep their hands off you?" he sighed. Just by gyrating his hips against this man he'd had a mancrush on for decades, he'd instantly brought himself to the brink of coming. *Must slow down. Must. Slow down.* He nipped at Steffen's lower lip. He swept his hand up Steffen's hard abdomen, slinking a couple fingers between two buttons to revel in the hairy, well-developed chest.

Amadeo's sensitive fingertips felt Steffen's heart beating wildly. When Amadeo covered Steffen's mouth with his own and slowly, sensuously sucked the lower lip into his mouth, Steffen parted his own lips, too. An enormous shudder wracked Amadeo's entire body, rolling through him like an earthquake from head to toe. He had his heart's desire in his hands. And the other man wasn't pounding him into a pulp.

Steffen kissed him back, his heated snorts coming short and fast against the side of Amadeo's face. Amadeo lapped his tongue against the backs of Steffen's teeth and dared to plunge his fingers farther beneath the sopping shirt fabric. When he found the nubbin of the nipple and pinched, Steffen gasped into his mouth.

And shoved him away with his free hand.

"What the hell's wrong with you, you fucking pervert?" Steffen strained at his bond, but his free hand scrabbled to clutch Amadeo's shirtfront.

Amadeo had stepped out of reach and now had his hands held up in a surrender gesture. "Dude! Accept my apologies! I'm sorry if I misinterpreted—"

"Misinterpret my ass!" roared Steffen. "We were just talking about *bondage clubs*, you dirtbag! I wasn't expecting you to get all up in my grill."

Amadeo remained contrite. “Apologies! I got carried away, I admit.” He dared to gesture to Steffen grandly, as though presenting a washer and dryer on a game show. “But look at this. Can you blame me? Dude. You’re one smoking-hot sex machine. I’m sorry. You must get that all the time. I apologize if I treated you like an object. I was just carried away by the heat of the moment, talking about bondage and all.”

His apologies—and flattery—worked. The fire was dying from Steffen’s eyes, and he no longer snorted like a lathered horse. He didn’t even seem to notice that one of his wrists was still cuffed to the wall, and the bulge in his crotch had not gone down one centimeter. Amadeo had never been more aroused in his life, with this fine, fuckable quarterback bound to his tack room wall. Steffen was sweating so profusely in the hundred-degree-plus room his denim button-down shirt was plastered to his chest. Amadeo wanted to drop to his knees and lick the salt from between those meaty pecs.

Steffen’s tone had lost most of its anger. “Listen. I’m straight. That’s just the way it is. I’ve been to the Racquet Club, but I’ve only played with a few ladies. I’m a ladies’ man all the way, pal.”

Amadeo dared to approach his old high school mate within punching range. Steffen had dropped his hand to his side now, and he merely looked a bit exasperated. “I understand. I just misread your cues. Most men who go to the club bat for both teams. Most men want to swing both ways to get the maximum enjoyment from the scene.”

Steffen squinted at Amadeo. “You swing both ways?”

“Sure. I love a good muff-diving like the next guy, and who doesn’t like to be edged by that Mistress Tiffany at the club, am I right?”

They were practically back-slapping buddies now, Amadeo could tell. “Okay,” Steffen admitted, “maybe I’ve been groped by a few guys, but who hasn’t. I’m no bugger.”

Who hasn't? Men who don't enjoy that sort of thing, that's who hasn't. Amadeo must proceed with tact. Now he stepped so close to the quarterback their boners nearly touched again. "Sure, who hasn't? You're drunk one night, there are no chicks around, some hot guy comes onto you…"

"Exactly."

Steffen barely flinched when Amadeo grabbed a nice handful of his bulging dick. "A man needs release. Doesn't really matter who gives it to him. He just closes his eyes and goes with the sensation. It's a manly thing, needing release. Women don't need release like men do. Men get all backed up and cranky if they don't come all the time."

Steffen practically laughed now, although Amadeo was expertly massaging his penis. "Blue balls."

"Right. Men need a good, old-fashioned, mind-blowing orgasm pretty much all the time." It truly was a pleasure standing this close to his idol, breathing in his musky scent. Steffen Jung was literally woodsy, as though he'd been doing carpentry work. And, of course, the slab of meat filling Amadeo's palm was making him wild with lust.

"Exactly." Steffen put his free hand on his hip, as though afraid he might do something else with it. He was going to be one of those men who pretended "it" wasn't happening, Amadeo could tell. That was fine with him.

Now Steffen allowed Amadeo to lick his jaw line. "Then you won't mind if I take your long, fat dick into my mouth." Silence. Pulling back, Amadeo touched the tip of his crooked Roman nose to Steffen's straight Teutonic one. Steffen's eyelids quivered and nearly slid shut when Amadeo's thumb rubbed his cock's corona. Amadeo just knew when he got to his knees he would see a little wet spot there on the jeans. "I'll take that as a no. You don't mind."

And he got to his knees.

Steffen gasped when Amadeo mouthed the delicious meat—the wet spot—through the jean material. Exhaling, he imbued the entire cock with warmth, and it pulsed enticingly against his lips. He couldn't waste a second in his seduction of this tasty stud, and his experienced fingers were already flying to undo Steffen's belt buckle.

Ah. He mouthed the fat cock and balls through the boxer briefs but couldn't wait to hitch his fingers under the elastic and watch the lengthy penis pop out. When he buried his face in the steamy crotch, inhaling deeply of the masculine, oaky scent, Steffen actually touched the top of Amadeo's head. Steffen was acquiescing. He even spread his feet far apart on the floor to show his submission to Amadeo. He wove his fingers through Amadeo's hair and even angled his hips at the other man.

Amadeo twined his tongue around the base of the muscular, veined cock. He lovingly palmed the cockhead, already slick with jism. This was what Amadeo had dreamed of for decades. His mouth watered and he opened wide to take one pebbled testicle into his mouth. Steffen's hips twitched as he humped Amadeo's hand, the air. It was too good to be true that he was finally suckling at the balls he'd seen swaying so alluringly in that high school locker room before Steffen had soaped them so thoroughly.

Now Steffen's hand gripped Amadeo's skull, urging him to suck his prick. Steffen gasped and grunted as Amadeo tongued his balls. Amadeo was surprised to hear the virile football player snarl so commandingly. "Suck my dick."

Amadeo obliged. *Enough of the teasing*. He finally had that tasty meat down his throat, and he put his all into it. He hoovered the length of that colossal meat down his throat, using his throat muscles to massage it. His tongue described fancy curlicues up and down the underside of the pulsating cock. He sucked with such enthusiasm that within a few moments Steffen was gasping with the strangled noises of a man on the edge.

"Oh, God. Oh, God. *Oh, God.*"

"Mm." Amadeo knew that his appreciative murmuring would vibrate through Steffen's straining penis. The urethra bubbled with the roiling semen that was fixing to explode. Amadeo hummed and grunted as he pistoned his head back and forth. He knew his unbridled, bestial sounds added to the lewd, forbidden excitement of the moment. Steffen released a gratifying gusher of jism down his throat.

Steffen's thighs bunched up so tightly they were like marble pillars. Amadeo gulped to contain the volume of seed spurting forth. The big cock twitched and pulsed with delicious life. Now he relaxed a little and savored the flavor. *Big football player must be a vegetarian.* As a cattle rancher and avid cocksucker, Amadeo was familiar with the taste of a meat-eating load of semen.

Lost in the bliss of the moment, Amadeo gulped and moaned while wrapping his arms around the naked, sinewy hips. He ran his palms down the velvety slope of Steffen's lower back. How many times had he imagined doing exactly this against the backdrop of the locker room? Steffen would stand with spread feet spearing that beautiful penis down Amadeo's throat. Amadeo would swallow every drop of his tasty load. In these scenarios, every other boy melted away from the fringes of Amadeo's awareness. He was no longer the guitar-playing minority stoner on the outside looking in, but a worthy participant. A receptacle worthy of receiving such a delicious, holy load.

He had barely finished rimming the slit with his tongue-tip when Steffen shoved him away violently. Amadeo slid on his ass, stunned and hurt. "Uncuff me," Steffen growled menacingly. Then he tried with one hand to stuff away his long hose of a cock that dangled, purplish and shiny.

"Of course." Amadeo had to briefly wonder where the keys for those cuffs were. Like Steffen, he had about a hundred keys on a ring at his waist. Then he remembered. Keys for every apparatus in this room were in a pocket inside the tack trunk.

Steffen huffed angrily as Amadeo uncuffed him. Once free, he swiftly walked to the door, finishing buttoning his jeans with his back to Amadeo. Amadeo was sad it had to end this way, but at least now he'd have a real memory instead of some groping teenaged imagining.

Still, he tried. "Steffen—"

Steffen spun about and pointed at the ground. "*Mister* Jung to you, buddy!"

Amadeo wasn't about to kowtow. He was a Dom in the lifestyle, and he called no one Mister. "Steffen, I'm not sorry I just sucked your cock. I'd do it again in a hot minute."

Steffen didn't even seem to be listening. "No. No." He jabbed a forefinger at some saddle or other. "This? *Never happened.*" And he spun back on a boot heel and stormed out the door.

Unshed tears stung Amadeo's eyes, but he remained stoic. It *had* happened, after all. He had just drained the penis of the football quarterback. And the quarterback had responded enthusiastically.

Steffen could pretend all he wanted that it had never happened. But how would he react the next time he set eyes on Amadeo?

Chapter Four

"Oh, *please*, Jaclyn! That guy was so cheap he had a flask of gin in his pocket!" The two women sat at a corner table in the Cavern on the Green vaguely overseeing the installation of the floor linoleum. Willow had chosen a fake rock pattern that she hoped would give the cafe that rubbly, Flintstones look. "And he looked everywhere *but* at the check when it arrived."

Jaclyn defended her choice of a double date for Willow. "Robin *is* a very thrifty man, Willow. That can be a *good* quality in a man, not a negative one. How else do you think he saved enough to purchase his beautiful home?"

Willow snorted and stirred her chocolate milk with her straw. "Well, I haven't seen his beautiful home. I'm sure he's got glow-in-the-dark stars on the ceiling and Star Wars sheets on his bed."

"What?"

"Didn't you hear him talking about his ghost busting society? He seriously goes around looking for ghosts."

Jaclyn held her pinkie out as she sipped her coffee from the Styrofoam cup. "Oh, I believe that's some very high-minded paranormal society."

Willow made a face of exasperation. "Jaclyn. Please. He had a *proton pack* in his car."

"That's some highly scientific instrument that records sensitive data that the human ear can't pick up. Anyway, Willow. You really blew it by talking about your ex. You know you're not supposed to talk about your ex on a date."

"*I* blew it? Like I care? Jaclyn, Matt was my *world* for eight years. I can hardly avoid the subject. Besides. Your Robin the Great and Magnificent asked me how long I'd been divorced. I told him. Not yet."

"Any day now, right? How upset was Matt to hear about your sweet dog?"

Willow squeezed her eyes shut and blew bubbles into her milk through the straw. Frankly, if it weren't for meeting that stunning and chiseled building inspector yesterday, the entire day would've been an utter loss. Steffen Jung had thrown her for such a loop she had even confided in him her darkest most erotic secret—the scene she'd witnessed at Daytona Beach during spring break. That Steffen was experienced in the use of the St. Andrew's Cross had turned Willow on so heavily she had broken out her old vibrator last night. That vibrator was so ancient it sounded like she was chipping wood in her upstairs motel suite, but she didn't care how many carpet installers heard her.

That building inspector with the seductive grin had rustled some long-forgotten libido in her. Things had been so bad with Matt for years before she had left, she had really not been stimulated by another man in ages. Then this chiseled drink of water with the Irish accent loped into her motel and had her confessing that she had masturbated thinking of one man sucking another's cock. *It was the fault of that damned menu I found. I seriously want to enact a Horse and Buggy with Steffen Jung...whatever that is.* In fact, she now had the menu secreted in her enormous laptop carryall sitting next to her on the upholstered bench seat. Steffen had said he would return today. Something about HVAC, she couldn't exactly recall. She'd been too busy watching his luscious ass as he left. She was determined to show him the menu, if only to pretend it was a fine example of Desert Modern printing.

"Matt wasn't very upset, listen, where'd you find that Ronnie Dobbs character? He was a piece of work."

"Oh, he came by? What do you mean, piece of work? He's…ah, I believe he's some associate of Fernando's." Fernando was allegedly some sort of handyman. Willow had never seen Fernando be handy at anything other than a remote control, so she couldn't vouch for that.

"Jaclyn, seriously. Is Ronnie Dobbs a monster truck friend of Fernando's? Because I could really see that. This guy was really beyond the beyond."

"What makes you think he must be a monster truck friend? All I know is he claimed to know for a fact that Norman Fell's watch was in here somewhere."

"Well, I don't see where that would be that valuable, Jaclyn, unless Norman happened to inscribe it with his name. Well, luckily that building inspector was here when Ronnie showed up. He scared the whackjob away. I really hope he never comes around again, even *if* we find that stupid watch. He gave me the creeps." Willow sighed deeply. "Jaclyn, I kid you not. That inspector was the steamiest thing I've seen since…Well, maybe *ever*."

Jaclyn's eyes widened and she scooted closer. "Really? Which building inspector? I'm sure I know him."

That hadn't occurred to Willow that Jaclyn would know Steffen. Of course she would, being a realtor. "Steffen Jung. He—"

Willow had the words startled right out of her when Jaclyn slammed the tabletop with her palm. Jaclyn looked to the ceiling for assistance. "Steffen Jung? What a player!" Only she pronounced it "play-uh."

"What do you mean? You mean, like, he gets around?"

"Gets around? He gets around out of town! That guy is a regular womanizer. Of *course* he is, look at him! He's drop-dead gorgeous." Jaclyn waved her hand in front of her own face as though sprinkling fairy dust. "He's got those white teeth, that perpetual five-o'clock perfect shadow, that whole Green Lantern thing going on."

"He was a test pilot?" Unfortunately, Willow knew her superheroes from being married to Matt.

"What? No, I mean he looks like Ryan Reynolds, only more buff. And you wonder why he's never been married? I'm always suspicious of men who have never been married by the time they hit age forty. Like, what's wrong with them if they're not gay? And Steffen Jung is definitely not gay."

"Thanks for vouching for me, Jaclyn."

Both women gasped and jumped in their seats. Willow saw by Jaclyn's startled face that Steffen Jung stood right behind her. Gripping the edge of the table, Willow slowly swiveled. Her eyes met Steffen's belt buckle first, unintentionally eyeing his package cradled in a fresh pair of 501s. *Oh, God. I'm the manizer. I'm the one objectifying him, treating him like a gorgeous piece of meat. Which he is.* Forcing an innocent smile onto her face, she looked into his dazzling eyes. Luckily, he had a good sense of humor.

"Oh!" said Jaclyn, flustered. "Hi, Steffen. Oh, don't mind us. We were just talking about the lack of available men in this town. Saying that, ah, you were one of the only ones. You're not married, right?"

"Right. Came close a couple times, but never took the plunge. And you're right. I'm not gay."

"Oh, ha-ha," said Jaclyn in a bad attempt at being light. "Just commitment-shy."

Willow wanted to sink into her newly rocky floor. She had to seize control of the situation. "We were just discussing this horrible blind date Jaclyn set me up on last night. He brought his own booze to the restaurant and he had a jet pack in his back seat."

Steffen said happily, "All right! A forward-thinking kind of guy. Don't tell me you're not racing to repeat the experience, Willow. And women wonder why they never have second dates."

Willow laughed with relief that Steffen was taking everything so casually—and that he now knew for a fact she was single. "Shall we go look at those kitchen vents? Or whatever you want to see first."

"Sure." Steffen even held out a hand for her to take, to help her stand. "But Jaclyn, I've got to harass you about that Ronnie Dobbs character you sent over here. He's a bit unhinged, to say the least." To Willow he said, "I ran his plates and license number, and he's right, he probably *is* the most arrested man in the Coachella Valley. Stuff like aggravated assault, drunk driving of course, drunk in public—mostly stuff a man would do while high or plain crazy, like climbing to the top of the Zippy Super Car Wash sign and resisting arrest. He actually had a show similar to *Cops* following him around, just on the assumption he'd get arrested again."

Willow asked, "Is there any truth to the spousal abuse he hinted at?"

A shadow darkened Steffen's face. "Yeah. Maybe ten arrests for that. Jaclyn, where'd you find this guy?"

Willow crossed her arms. "Let me guess. A monster truck rally."

"Hey, don't blame the messenger!" Standing, Jaclyn held her palms out. "I thought I was doing Willow a favor. All Fernando said was he had a friend who collected entertainment memorabilia from the fifties and sixties."

Steffen said, "Well, do Willow a favor and call that rabid guy off, will you? Because *I* am calling the *real* cops if I see him around here again." Taking Willow by the elbow as she shouldered her heavy bag, he told Jaclyn over his shoulder, "And tell Fernando that his insulation on the Rancho Mirage job isn't up to spec. He'll have to rip it out and start all over again."

Steffen was gentlemanly, waiting for her to pick her way through unfinished spaces of flooring as they headed for the glass doors of the Cavern on the Green. She held his arm close to her bosom, elated beyond belief that they were alone. "You're a taskmaster." Willow shuddered at the naughty double entendre of her words.

He looked down at her. "I try to be."

Her nipples stiffened at his double meaning, too. She had worn a kicky summer dress—straps, a shirred bodice, and a flirty skirt. She knew she could not cover up her ample figure. In this heat, she would just look crazy if she wore long sleeves. She had never been able to lose the weight she'd gained when she'd quit smoking five years earlier, so she would have to live with it. Any potential lover deserved honesty in advertising, anyway. "I have something to show you, something I found. And I refrained from going inside the Cesar Romero Room until you showed up. I knew you'd want to see it, too. The carpenter hasn't unstuck the front door, but we can go in from the utility room."

"That's incredibly thoughtful! What'd you find?"

"I'll show you once we're inside."

While Willow unlocked the utility room connecting door, she said, "I have to apologize for Jaclyn. You know how racy women can get when they're together. We shouldn't have been discussing your sexual orientation or dating history."

"Why the hell not? I know *exactly* how racy women can get, and that's part of what I love about them. In fact, I have a proposal for you. But I think I should wait until we're out on a proper date to make the proposition."

A proper date? Willow had the door open a few inches but was so stunned she just froze for a few seconds. *Did I just hear correctly? He wants a proper date with me? But wait...Jaclyn said—*

He butted into her thoughts. "As far as me having never married, I did come close a couple of times. I'm not a *completely* callous bastard. And the rumors of my skirt-chasing have been greatly exaggerated. I think you might be pleasantly surprised by how polite I can be. Can you take enough time off the Searchlight to let me take you to the Frank Sinatra House?"

Actually, Willow had heard about that place. Last night, after her session with her noisy old wood chipper, she had surfed for some of the architects Steffen probably loved, such as Neutra, Cody, and Frey. "That would be fun. I'd like to see that Kupka House that Neutra designed," she ventured to say. "Or that bank that Williams designed."

"There are all sorts of places we could go."

Steffen couldn't mask the excitement in his voice, and Willow knew she'd hit the nail right on the head with her architectural offer. Meeting Steffen had given her a whole new lease on life. Hearing his ideas for a date, she hadn't been this thrilled to the core in years. Not even purchasing the run-down motel had given her this sort of spine-tingling, adventurous turn-on. As she opened the door to the Cesar Romero Room, she was quite literally opening the door on a new life.

"Holy cow."

Willow knew that "cow" wasn't Steffen's first choice of word, but he was trying to remain civil for her. All she saw was a darkened room full of bulky furniture, so she went to pull the drapes. "Why, what is it?" Stark, crisp light reflected from the San Jacinto Mountains imbued the room like a stage, revealing upholstered furniture in sensuous shapes.

"Well, this here is a spanking bench." Steffen put his hand on a piece of furniture that resembled a pommel horse or a children's picnic table. Like the cross, it had obviously been homemade. Padded, and with different platforms for kneeling or resting various limbs, it matched the heart-shaped bed's headboard down to the same burgundy brocade fabric and brass upholstery nails. "This doesn't look much used either. This is a great find, Willow."

Willow was savvy enough to know about the cat o' nine tails she removed from a peg on the wall. She swished it about as though she knew what she was doing. "You know what we should do?" She looked naughtily at Steffen from beneath her bangs. "There's a separate unit out back by the pétanque court. I was remodeling it to charge more for it, you know, a separate cottage and all."

Steffen's eyes shined with excitement. He obviously already got her drift. "We move all of this equipment out there."

"Right. Hell, we could even call *that* the Cesar Romero Cottage, although I'd have to change the name plate." She whipped the crushed velvet bedspread with the cat o'nine tails, feeling deliciously sinful.

Steffen approached her, his hands hovering over her shoulders. "No, don't move the name plate. Have you named the cottage yet? Seeing you just now gave me an idea."

Willow stood back and experimentally whipped the bed again. "Oh, yeah? What?"

"The Gadabout Gaddis Cottage."

All of her senses were alive. A shiver swept up and down her spine, her torso, like those electrical jars in Dr. Frankenstein's lab. "Why's that?"

"Gadabout Gaddis was a television fisherman in the old days. I used to see reruns of his show as a kid in Ireland. He was just a real down-to-earth guy, always tossing his cigarette butts into the undergrowth when he got out of a boat. He used to vacation in Palm Springs. And you looked like a fly fisherman just now, flicking that whip." He wiggled an eyebrow. "Quite a voluptuous and shapely fisherman."

Not knowing whether to be complimented or insulted, Willow giggled. "Gadabout Gaddis sounds like one of the implements used in this room, anyway. Isn't a gadabout sort of a man about town, a bon vivant?"

"I think it's someone who is in the social whirl, yeah. But what would you *do* with the Gadabout Gaddis Cottage? You said you didn't want this to be 'that sort of establishment.'"

Willow batted her eyelashes as she ran the falls through the *O* she made of her fingers. "It's a woman's prerogative to change her mind. I could always just save it, set it aside, rent it out to *select* people."

Steffen's eyes flickered out the window briefly, and he got a faraway look. "I think I may know a few of those people."

"I'm sure you do. Now what's this?" With the whip, Willow tapped another piece of furniture that resembled a sawhorse, but upholstered like the other furniture with brass nails.

"This is more of a discipline stand. See? There are D-rings to attach cuffs, bonds. A *person* could kneel like this." Steffen kneeled on the lowest bar, allowing his arms to dangle over the body of the sawhorse.

Willow's opportunity was clear as an unmuddied lake. Steffen was displaying his curvaceous ass, and she held a whip. However, that was bit too bold, even for as many strides as she'd been making in getting away from Matt, moving toward something new. So she kneeled on the padded support on the opposite side, also dangling her arms over the horse. Their arms intertwined, and they stared unabashed at each other.

Steffen said, "I think some people might call it a fuck bench."

There was no denying that their hearts were intertwined at that moment, too. Willow couldn't remember later whether she had made the first move, or Steffen. But all of a sudden they were kissing heatedly. It felt so right, although she hadn't kissed another man in years. It felt natural to move her lips over his, to smack and make loud kissing noises, like some kind of starving animal.

Steffen's natural woodsy scent rose up and infused her skin when she ran her palm over his closely-shaven head. The upholstered wooden bars prevented them from doing much more than feast on each other's mouths, but Willow never wanted to let him go. She hadn't realized until now how much she had missed embracing a man, a real man. He kissed her tenderly, not plunging his tongue into her mouth like an oyster slider, as she recalled so many fumbling men doing.

Steffen held her head softly, massaging her skull with his fingertips. Although he licked her lips lightly, she could feel the tremor in his fingers, his ragged breathing. *He's turned on. He wants me*. She dared to break the kiss and pepper his sculpted chin and jaw line with wet, noisy kisses.

She realized she was panting, too. Steffen sank his fingers deeper into her hair, vigorously rubbing her skull as he strove to taste her throat. Willow's ample tits just barely cleared the top bar of the fuck bench so she rested them there, displayed like a horny lowland bird's plumage, plump and half-exposed. When Steffen lowered his head to taste the pit of her throat, a high-pitched sigh escaped her, startling her. Her pussy quivered when he applied a flat tongue to her clavicle, and she wanted nothing more than for him to suck a nipple into his mouth, to nibble it between his teeth.

She panted so rapidly she was getting light-headed. She ran her palms over his soft, brushy hair, cradling his face to her bosom. "Oh, Steffen," she sighed, and the shock of hearing her own voice scared her.

She must have leaped to her feet, because suddenly she was standing by the window, panting onto the glass, steaming it. "Oh, my," she breathed. "Oh, my."

Over at the fuck bench, Steffen held his head in his hands, probably incredulous that she had cut him off. Now she felt horrible. She knew men didn't like to be rejected—to get blue balls. While it had been easy enough to tear herself away from Robin the Great and Magnificent the night before, now she only wanted to take Steffen into her arms again, to soothe him, to suck his cock.

Instead she sat casually on the edge of the crushed velvet bedspread. She noticed her pussy was so juicy she sat on a wet spot, and she was glad the skirt of her summer dress was flowered. She willed her breathing to slow down. She relaxed both hands, palms toward the ceiling, on each of her knees, as though meditating.

She welcomed this new life. She embraced it and allowed it to unfold for her. She had been discouraged, frustrated, seeing the negative in everything. Steffen was giving her new hope, goodness, potential.

Eventually her breathing slowed enough for her to inquire, "What was your proposal?"

She couldn't wait for a proper date to find out.

Chapter Five

Exhaling, Steffen moved from a kneeling to a sitting position. He threaded his long legs through the legs of the discipline stand, draping his arms over the top wearily.

He didn't want Willow to know how disappointed he was she'd broken the kiss. He'd known she would be a hard nut to crack. He didn't even necessarily *want* her to be easy. Willow Paige being easy would be…well, too easy. He already had more appreciation for her, being a challenge. He meant every word when he said he wanted to take her on a real date, to a nice dinner, see some of the buildings he admired. He thought she might admire them, too, seeing as how she was remodeling a Desert Modern motel.

He didn't like that the women thought of him as a ladies' man. He had actually lived with a couple of women he hoped to marry—one of them a domineering top in bed, which was where he'd learned the ropes. But nothing had ever seemed to work out. It wasn't for lack of trying. Well, maybe he was a bit slow to commit. His globe-trotting childhood had maybe made him suspicious of a stable life where nothing changed. He was suspicious of the six o'clock dinner on the table, the routine, the sameness.

As a swinging bachelor, of course nothing was ever the same. Willow and Jaclyn were right about that much—he did have a different woman for every night of the week. Why not? It was all on the up and up. Everything had been fine until he'd met Miss Willow Paige. Suddenly he wanted something more substantial with her. She seemed to represent a fine balance between routine and excitement. For the first time, Steffen could imagine having dinner at six o'clock with her when he came home from work…and then strapping her to the St. Andrew's Cross in the Gadabout Gaddis Cottage.

But of course he was disappointed when Willow broke the kiss. He was a man. Kissing her was the most arousing experience since—well, since yesterday in Mr. Barbieri's tack room, but he wasn't prepared to discuss that, yet.

"What was your proposal?"

Her question forced him to remember yesterday. Having his cock sucked by that perverted cowboy had been all sorts of wrong—and right in so many ways. He'd felt an erotic rush of power, oddly, at being cuffed and powerless. How could one feel power while being physically powerless? Was it because he knew he was turning the other one on with his writhing, his false protests? He only had one wrist cuffed, after all, and both legs were free. He could have kickboxed that caveman vaquero to kingdom come.

How *dare* he, after all? Was Steffen giving off some weird pheromone he wasn't aware of? What made that—admittedly built, studly, and manly—poofter think that he was similarly inclined? Or did Barbieri make it a habit to corner strange men in his tack room and inhale their cocks down his throat? Of course, Steffen had been approached by men before. It was flattering. He'd be insulted if he'd never been groped in a club by another man. A couple of times, he'd been offered blow jobs while on the job to make certain code infractions go away. But never—never—had another man cuffed him to a wall bracket and practically *forced* an orgasm upon him!

But contrary to what he'd told Barbieri as he'd angrily stormed away, he *did* want it to happen again. And he'd been thinking about it ever since. "Proposal? Oh, something I've been thinking of since, ah, since I inspected that ranch last night. Remember?"

"Yes, you said you had to get over to, was it the Lone Palm Ranch?"

"Right, that's it. Well, I—" Steffen started to rise, to explain his idea.

Willow made the "stay" motion with her palm, and took a seat on the other side of the fuck bench. She intertwined her legs with Steffen's, and they leg wrestled to gain dominance. Was it possible Willow was a natural Domme and didn't know it? That would be difficult. *Someone* had to be on the bottom.

Up close and more intimate now, Steffen's idea sounded more and more ridiculous. "Well, I met the ranch owner, a Mr. Barbieri. I used to deal with his dad, but I guess his dad is getting too old, so the son's taken over." Willow listened patiently, her eyes unblinking. "And he, ah, this Mr. Barbieri, I thought he seemed like your type."

He didn't expect *that* level of pain in her eyes! Steffen was instantly sorry he'd said that! Now he gripped her forearms and held them tightly. "I didn't mean it that way, Willow. Hear me out. This has to do with your fantasy. The two men in Daytona Beach, remember?"

Pshew! Her eyes softened. She was willing to listen now, although he still felt incredibly awkward. He'd never made a proposition like this to anyone.

"I was thinking, maybe you'd like to sit in on a session…" He really didn't know how to finish. He looked out the window as though he'd see the answer in some skywriting.

She squeezed his hands and helped him out. "You mean watch? You'd like to help me with my *voyeuse* fantasies?"

An immense wave of relief washed over Steffen. "Yes, that's it! I could tell you were a *voyeuse*, that you enjoy watching, so I thought I could help you out, to reenact your experience in Daytona Beach!"

Now she was clearly thrilled. She squeezed his hands in her excitement, and sat so far forward her lovely breasts swelled over the upholstered bench. "Well, how could you *tell* that has been my fantasy for years? I only raved on and on about it, much to my mortification. Oh *God*, Steffen! Last night when I remembered telling you that, I was thoroughly *mortified!* How could I have told a complete stranger my most intimate desires?"

"Well, no worries there, Willow. I'm flattered you confided in me."

"And you're willing to help me by..."

Willow apparently didn't understand what he was driving at. Neither did he, since he hadn't asked Mr. Barbieri whether or not he'd participate in such a scheme in the first place. Yes, it *was* a completely harebrained scheme with almost zero chance of actually occurring. Maybe Steffen was only offering the idea to Willow as a way of getting his cock sucked by that strapping cowboy again. A brief imagining of Willow watching him get his cock sucked went flashing through his mind. His prick would be hanging, heavy and full. The cockhead would be shiny, ready to burst as Barbieri gripped his penis in his fist. Barbieri's mouth opened hungrily, sensuously...Steffen shuddered thinking of this possibility, and the shudder turned into a rush of lust that stiffened his cock again and filled his balls with seed.

"Well, this Mr. Barbieri—"

"What's his first name?"

Steffen frowned. He could he have blocked that out?

Willow assured him, "That's not important. Tell me your plan. How does it involve the rancher?"

"Well, he's got sort of, ah, homosexual leanings. I think he swings both ways, actually. And he's *very* good-looking. Italian, obviously. But picture a giant, six foot five Roman god with muscles so bulging his shirt buttons pop off."

Willow giggled. "You're *kidding*. That sounds positively delicious, Steffen. But tell me, how do *you* know he has homosexual leanings?"

This was the difficult part. It was one thing for a woman to have wild fantasies. A zipless fuck, so to speak, a fantasy that should remain in that realm. To enact fantasies sometimes meant their ruin. But Steffen knew, he knew with every cell in his body, that he wanted to continue playing with the rancher. It was perverted, it was twisted, but so be it. Willow might turn away, might be offended, might want Steffen all to herself, but that was the risk he had to take. This was her chance to have her erotic dreams realized.

"Well, he sort of, ah, *grabbed* me, and—"

He was saved by a brief knock on the door. One rap, that was it, but it was enough to divert their attention. This would give him enough time to gather his thoughts as Willow rose and went to Cesar Romero's door.

"Who is it? This door doesn't open."

Ronnie Dobbs. Steffen rose too, and moved her aside. "Yeah, who is it?"

"Amadeo Barbieri. Steffen? Is that you?"

"Yeah. Hey, come through the utility room next door. I'll meet you in there."

Willow followed at his heels like an eager puppy. "Is that him? The rancher? Amadeo is his name? What does he want over here? Did you already tell him about my fantasy?"

When Steffen stopped walking, Willow bumped into him. He gripped her by the shoulders. "Don't worry—I would never betray your confidence. I didn't tell him. It was just an idea that occurred to me—"

"Tell me what?"

Amadeo Barbieri was in the utility room, literally larger than life. Steffen was a relatively tall guy, about six one, but Barbieri loomed even larger. He still wore those chaps that buttoned up the sides and nestled his impressive cock and balls in the crotch of his jeans, and today he even slapped a cowboy hat against his powerful thigh. His father may have been an old school Italian, but Amadeo was all-American down to his leather vest and cowboy boots. Steffen wouldn't have been surprised if Amadeo had ridden a horse up here.

Steffen tried to save the day. "Tell you how much the St. Andrew's Cross was appraised for." He remembered that Amadeo had said something about wishing to purchase Willow's cross for the Racquet Club.

Willow looked confused, but Amadeo strode right over to the contraption and put his hands on his hips, assessing it. Then he rattled one of the cross-braces. "Looks well-constructed. Nicely padded, too."

"Oh, excuse me. Amadeo, this is Miss Willow Paige. She owns the Searchlight." As the two shook hands, Steffen continued, "I believe we just decided she doesn't want to sell the cross, though, unfortunately. She's got other plans for it." He examined Willow for signs of her approval of Amadeo, but one could never tell with women. They could be smiling and bestowing favor on some guy they wouldn't give the time of day to.

"Yes," Willow said brightly, "we decided to stash the cross and all the other bondage junk in the Gadabout Gaddis Cottage."

Amadeo laughed incredulously. "Gadabout Gaddis? Hey, wasn't he that TV fisherman from the old days who used to throw his cigarette butts—"

Steffen started to laugh. Amadeo had a playful side that he enjoyed. He wasn't chagrined about not being able to purchase the cross, or intrigued to know what other "bondage junk" Willow referred to. No, he was more interested in an amiable old fly fisherman.

"Willow." Suddenly Jaclyn was poking her head in the door, waving her cell phone. "I've got Fernando on the line. He's got some news you might want to hear."

"Oh," said Willow pertly. She looked at Amadeo. "Excuse me. I'm sorry about the cross. We just came up with this new idea just now. Yesterday I would've been glad to sell it to you. I'll be right back." Willow went into the hallway and took the phone from Jaclyn.

Amadeo raised an eyebrow. "New idea? Are you planning to give the Racquet Club a run for its money? It's only four blocks away."

Steffen wasn't prepared for the enormous impact just standing next to Amadeo had on him. While of course his cock had erected when he had kissed the shapely Miss Paige, now a tingle of a more forbidden nature now swept through his pecker and balls. He felt as though he knew what was on this strapping buck's mind as he crossed his arms. It did look as though Amadeo had popped a couple of shirt buttons just on the strength of those bulging pecs alone. His chest looked shaven, too, creamy and hairless. Steffen reddened to know he'd been caught looking at another man's chest.

"No, no, just some new idea to remodel a separate cottage. Come in here."

"Whoa!" Amadeo grinned widely in appreciation of the burgundy brocade room. Even the walls were lined with a dark gold-flocked paper that made even a teetotaler like Steffen want to shake up a martini. "Ole Cesar Romero's been up to the devil's work. Nice spanking bench."

"Well, I don't think we *know* this was Cesar's room for sure," Steffen said. "Willow just decided to call it that. Listen, Amadeo." Now that he said the name aloud, it *did* sound familiar. Steffen couldn't place it. Amadeo's father Salvatore had no doubt mentioned his son's name before. "Listen. What do you think of Willow Paige? She's pretty, isn't she?"

Amadeo looked at Steffen, low and dark. "Bro. You don't have to warn *me* away from her. You saw her first. The spoils of victory and all that."

"No, that's not it. The thing is, we were talking yesterday before I went to your place. She mentioned a fantasy she'd had."

Amadeo moved closer, clearly intrigued. His ripe, sweaty scent wasn't out of line with what Steffen knew of him, his job. He'd been on a horse all morning. Of course he was sweaty and smelled of cowhide. "Fantasy, eh? Women do have the most interesting fantasies. What was it?"

"Well, ah…" Steffen should be accustomed to discussing prurient things frankly. He did it often—just with other women, not men. He got it out all in a rush. "She wants to see two men getting it on."

"Well, now," Amadeo said lewdly. He circled Steffen, examining him from all angles. His cowboy hat was slung from a corner of the spanking bench casually, as though he roamed in rooms like this all the time, which he probably did. "That *does* sound like a juicy proposal. And she wants to see us?"

"Well, I didn't get around to making a concrete proposition, although I did mention you, yeah."

"Did you mention what we did yesterday? Oh, wait. That never happened."

Steffen burned with both anger and embarrassment. "No. That's the part that might come as a shock to her. Listen, Amadeo. I just want to make her happy. I really value this woman. I want to make her dream come true."

Amadeo grabbed Steffen's jaw and held him tight. "Admit it. You enjoyed it."

Steffen wrapped his fingers around Amadeo's wrist but didn't yank the hand away. "I admit nothing, you asshole. I just want to make Willow happy."

Amadeo grinned with delight. "You just want me to suck your cock again. You just can't wait to sink your dick down another man's hot, hungry throat."

It was probably just Amadeo's dirty talk, but he was right—Steffen's cock lengthened and engorged against his thigh. "Doesn't matter to me who's doing the sucking. Long as it's good."

Amadeo let go of his jaw but still stared down at him, so close Steffen was slammed by his body heat. "Does it have to be that particular way to indulge her fantasy? Did she specify she wanted to see you get your cock sucked by a muscular cowboy?"

Steffen chuckled. "Of course not. She just saw two men in an alley once, one on his knees sucking the other."

Amadeo grinned now too. "So we'll turn the tables. That's what you learn in the lifestyle. Give people what they don't expect. Keep people on their toes. That's why I'm a switch."

"A switch?"

"I can switch between dominance and submission. Doesn't matter to me—it's whatever fits the particular scene we're in." Amadeo gripped Steffen's jaw again and planted a giant, openmouthed kiss on him. Steffen was surprised to find himself melting. Instead of being affronted or hauling off and punching the guy, he swooned into it, the way a woman would. He even clung to the lapels of Amadeo's leather vest and humped Amadeo's thigh like a dog.

Amadeo broke the kiss with a smacking sound. "Sometimes I like to suck cock. Sometimes I like to get sucked." He took Steffen's hand and pressed it to his hard-on, cradled so enticingly between the chaps. It was an alien feeling for Steffen, but not unwelcome. It was thrillingly foreign to have his hand cupping someone else's dick, and he reveled in the feeling, measuring the length with his palm, feeling that the breadth was less than his. He shivered when he humped the chaps-clad thigh. Knowing that Willow would bust back into the room at any moment made the naughty aura even more forbidden.

Amadeo grinned crookedly. "You like that, huh? You like squeezing my dick, don't you? Feels good to have your hand full of a nice stiff piece of meat. Here. Unbuckle my belt. Yeah, that's a three-dimensional image of my ranch brand, Lone Palm. *Ah.* That's right. Slide your hand into my crotch. No, I go commando."

Steffen was pleasantly surprised to find Amadeo naked under the erotic chaps and jeans. Salaciously, he rubbed the steamy pubic bone with his thumb, just brushing his fingertips against the moist, stiff root of his prick. Leaning back against the spanking bench, Amadeo slung one arm lazily behind his own head as though posing for *Men's Health*. He must know he made a stunning picture, the stud exposing his manhood for all to see. "Wrap your hand around my dick, Steffen. Do it. You know you want to feel it."

Steffen must have had a stubborn streak. As much as he wanted to fulfill Amadeo's command, he really wanted to know if his chest was waxed. Half-unbuttoning and half-tearing, he rent the checkered shirt so the meaty pecs were exposed. His eyes must have had a voracious look, for Amadeo sighed.

"Ah. You want to admire my chest. You want to suckle my nipple. Well, then. *Here*."

And he grabbed the back of Steffen's neck and smashed Steffen's face to his chest.

Chapter Six

Ah. It was heavenly to be admired, to be suckled by such a lean and formerly straight horndog as Steffen Jung.

Amadeo had spent all night last jacking off to the fresh memory of sucking this man's dick. Now he had somehow succeeded in seducing the building inspector into shoving his hand down Amadeo's pants. Steffen must *really* want to please that voluptuous motel owner. *Excellent.*

Men—and women—often wanted to nuzzle his buff, hairless chest. Yes, he had it waxed. There was nothing worse than those bearish men who used to climb all over him at the Racquet Club. Now that he waxed, he more often got the type of fellow he wanted—long, lean, and savory, like Steffen Jung.

Steffen suckled Amadeo's nipple experimentally. When he nibbled it between his incisors, Amadeo shuddered so heavily his other nipple erected, his chest breaking out into gooseflesh. Steffen wound his fingers through Amadeo's silken bush, and he tentatively fingered the rigid root of his cock. Amadeo's lips had measured Steffen's tool, and he knew he wasn't as impressive. Not many men were. But to a man who had never fingered another dick before, he knew Steffen was stunned by the immediacy, the pungency, the oily, veined length of it.

Steffen's groan vibrated the depth of Amadeo's chest as Steffen boldly smoothed his hand around the entire upper side of the cock, still sheathed in the jeans.

"You like that." Amadeo was almost tender now, although just seconds away from coming. He cradled the back of Steffen's skull, nuzzling Steffen's face against his smooth chest. "You like your hand being full of a big dick."

"Guys, I just talked to Fernando. He told me that Ronnie Dobbs was arrested for playing air guitar and eating some ant—*oh, my.*"

Both men froze in position. Steffen held his breath, Amadeo's nipple still between his teeth.

Amadeo barely knew Willow Paige. She was a newcomer to Last Chance, from all accounts a freshly divorced beauty who had suffered some sort of tragedy in Florida, no one seemed to know what. It must have had something to do with her despicable husband, for everyone was in agreement that he was a douche bag, a sort of coke-snorting wife beater. Whatever the case, Willow was no spring chicken, maybe a little over thirty, but had no children in tow. This led kinksters at the Racquet Club to speculate the tragedy had to do with a child. Small town people loved to talk. And they all wanted to know the lowdown on the little minx who had purchased the old Sunset Palomino Ranch. Amadeo knew his father had been a client here back in the day, but he shuddered to think of his father in the Cesar Romero Room.

Willow stood with her hand on the doorknob, the door that connected Cesar Romero's room to the utility room. Her mouth was a perfect *O*, and her overgrown bangs made her look younger than she probably was. Amadeo wondered if she often wandered around the construction site in those high-heeled sandals. Rubble was everywhere, yet she was practically dressed for a bondage club in a revealing "little black dress" that had bra cups made to order for her high, jiggly tits.

She placed a limp hand on her bosom now. "Oh, excuse me. I'll leave you alone."

"No!" both men shouted at once.

Amadeo gripped Steffen's hand from outside the jeans, to prevent him from removing it. He spoke hurriedly, so Steffen didn't get a chance to ruin things. "Steffen told me about your fantasy," he said kindly. "And we wanted to help you fulfill it."

The expression on her face made a sea change. From shock and embarrassment, her face took on an enlightened, knowing look. "Ah," she said, slowly smiling. "Yes, we talked about that. Don't stop, Steffen!" She came closer, shutting the connecting door behind her. "Mr. Barbieri—"

"Amadeo."

"Amadeo, I just didn't know you were such a swift operator." She perched on the seat of the spanking bench, crossing her knees, very ladylike. "Please. Don't mind me. Continue. What are you doing?"

Amadeo squeezed Steffen's hand inside the crotch of his jeans. The woman's gaze went directly to the length of cock that was exposed, the trunk of Amadeo's prick that Steffen was groping. Amadeo explained, "I'm just teaching Steffen here that there are many different ways of getting your kink on. Last night I sucked *his* cock. He spewed and spewed his delicious load into my mouth." Amadeo looked affectionately at the close-shaven head that he fondled to his chest. "Today I'm showing him the joys of being subservient, of servicing another man. Right, Steffen?"

"Right," Steffen mumbled, back to lapping up Amadeo's nipple.

"I'm a *voyeuse,*" Willow said, chipper as could be. "Am I going to be able to watch Steffen suck your penis?"

Amadeo assured her. "That's exactly what you're going to see. We aim to please, miss. Right, Steffen? Get off my teat. Get down on your fucking knees and *service* me."

"Oh, God," whispered Willow. She set her toes on the floor in order to lean forward, hands on knees. It sure looked as though she was rotating her pelvis on the upholstered corner of the spanking bench. Her black dress was a flimsy rayon affair, just enough material to buffer the upholstered rounded corner she gyrated her clit against.

What a nasty, sexy woman. Dear God. This man is going to be gulping my load in seconds if I don't slow him down. Steffen was so enthusiastic to suck his first dick Amadeo had to shove him by the shoulder so he fell back onto some sort of fuck bench. The piece of furniture matched the other pieces in the room. Now Steffen could perch about two feet off the floor, his thighs spread, his bulging erection plain for anyone to see. He couldn't pretend to his girlfriend he didn't want this. He clearly loved this motel owner, but it was also clearly not repellant to him to be lifting a cowboy's long penis from the stricture of his jeans.

Amadeo wasn't sure who to watch. Which was sexier? The woman grinding her labia against the corner of the bench, gyrating like a pole dancer, or the banging hot quarterback with his mouth open about to munch his cock?

"Steffen. Lick his cock like it's a candy cane."

Both men looked at Willow. It was so unexpected, her order. She looked like such a demure, prissy woman, for some reason. She had a clean-living way of speaking, as though all women from Florida were clean livers. Just her uttering the word "cock" aloud had both men frozen with shock. She stared at them as though they had toilet paper stuck to their shoes.

"What's wrong? What did I say? Cock?"

"Well, yeah," Amadeo admitted. "It sounds strange coming from you."

"Why coming from me? Cock, cock, cock! There, I said it! Now *you*—Steffen!" Willow even stood, sauntering toward the men with her arms crossed authoritatively. "Hold that big prick in your hand. Lick it all over, like a lollipop."

"Yes, ma'am."

When Steffen complied, Amadeo inadvertently gasped. He was used to receiving blow jobs from anonymous patrons at the Racquet Club, people he probably wouldn't associate with in real life. But he already knew he wanted to associate with Steffen. He actually liked the man, and wasn't just trying to get a stop work order lifted. For once, he could imagine seeing this man again and again. Steffen had a beautifully rounded ass just ripe for plowing, and Amadeo couldn't wait to see him shirtless. He admired the man's work ethic, his interest in architecture, and his general manliness.

"*Fuck.*" Steffen was flicking his tongue in and out of his cock's slit. It was beyond erotic to look down on his closely-shaven head and think, "This is the building inspector who wouldn't approve my work." Amadeo had played games involving similar scenes at the Racquet Club, the usual things where a cop pulled someone over for speeding, but one blow job later, naturally the cop let the speeder go.

The roles were lewdly reversed now, giving Amadeo some dirty ideas. "You like that, don't you, Mr. Building Inspector? You only inspected my rafters to find something wrong with them because you really wanted to suck my dick. You wanted me to watch your hard-on as you descended the ladder."

It was amazing how quickly Willow picked up on the game. Putting one hand on Amadeo's shoulder, she put the other on Steffen's. "Yes, Mr. Building Inspector. Did you give this good man some demerits in his tack room because you really couldn't wait to wrap your lips around his penis? You are one nasty man, Mr. Jung."

This dirty talk appeared to turn on Steffen, for he deep-throated Amadeo's prick, his lips meeting the base of the cock.

Gasping, Amadeo joined in the taunting. "Yeah. You want to swallow my long cock. You've been waiting for this your whole life. You've been wondering what it tastes like, having a long penis in your mouth."

Willow continued Amadeo's sentence. "It fills you, sucking that long, velvety cock." She caressed the back of Steffen's head, urging his face toward Amadeo's crotch. "Use your tongue. Squiggle your tongue back and forth as you lean into him."

Amadeo's fingers met Willow's when he tried to direct Steffen's head. Amadeo put some dominance into their talk. "You've wanted to taste a male member for so long, Steffen, haven't you? Ever since those high school days when you *knew* I was drooling for you. Mr.

Macho Quarterback with the perfect ass and chest, who *didn't* want you back then?"

Steffen paused, and looked up at Amadeo. Could it be this was the first time he had remembered seeing Amadeo in high school?

But Steffen detached his mouth long enough to utter, "Amadeo Barbieri. You're a crude ranch hand. But *I* know how to suck a cock like this." He inhaled Amadeo's long meat.

Willow wasn't immune to her boyfriend's words either. Suddenly, she stood behind Steffen with a cat o'nine tails brandished in her hand. *Does she know how to handle that?* It took stamina, talent, and lots of practice to land the falls of the cat o'nine tails correctly. And it left marks. Only a couple of professional women at the Racquet Club knew how to flex and tease with all nine of the tails.

Luckily, a much easier flogger was close at hand. Cesar Romero apparently came prepared for any such eventuality. Amadeo handed Willow the soft suede mop flogger. "This one's easier to handle," he explained. "It doesn't hurt, but you can get a lot sexier with it."

Willow looked down at her boyfriend eagerly hoovering Amadeo's meat. "Should I slow him down?"

"I've never seen him without his shirt. Strip him."

"Neither have I. But I've been dying to." Willow seductively did Amadeo's bidding. Crouching behind Steffen, she plastered her ample tits to his back and slowly unbuttoned his work shirt. Her eyes flickered between watching his shoulder revealed and watching Amadeo watch. "So beautiful," she breathed, revealing the other shoulder. Steffen had to let go of the cock for her to peel the cuff over his hand, but he kept eagerly sucking, putting his tongue into it.

"That's good, boy," Amadeo said approvingly, lovingly rubbing the brushy hair. He was seriously afraid he'd come before Willow got to stripping Steffen's pants and whipping his ass. Cesar had had the foresight to arrange many mirrors with elaborate gilt frames all about the room in aesthetic positions. Right now Willow's wide, shapely ass was reflected for Amadeo's pleasure as she ground her pussy against her boyfriend's lovely rounded ass. "Slow down. You're getting me too hot. Jack me, slowly. Willow has a surprise for you."

"You just can't control yourself, can't you?" Willow teased. Steffen's belt must have been so heavy with the hundred keys he had jangling there, the jeans easily fell to his knees, and Willow slipped a hand beneath the tight briefs to lower them, too. Another mirror off to the side revealed the spring of the well-hung cock Amadeo had loved with his mouth the night before. Willow fisted Steffen's juicy meat, and her words were anything but prim. "You like looking at this cowboy's big penis, don't you? You do know that Mommy's going to have to punish you for that. You just can't resist licking that cock, can you?"

Steffen's eyes were heavily lidded with lust. "No. I can't resist. I want to suck him till he comes and drink every drop. How are you going to punish me?"

"Your ass is mine. You know that, don't you?" Amadeo wished it was his hand smoothing over the beautifully rounded slope of Steffen's rump. The boy had game, that was for sure. He must've worked out quite often to have a build that cut, that defined. Amadeo's horseback riding was most of his workout, and the nonstop fence-building, cattle driving, branding, roping, and castra—well, it was more pleasant to watch Willow smacking that delicious ass with the mop flogger. "Spread your knees. Spread 'em so Mommy can slap your balls, too." Suspiciously expert, she gripped his meat while slapping his balls from behind. Amadeo knew the impact play of the mop flogger rarely hurt. It was always sexy to whip a fellow's cock and balls, and Steffen winced appropriately.

"Get his cock nice and purple, Mistress," Amadeo ordered. "And don't forget to lick my balls while Mommy is spanking you!"

"Oh, God, yes," Steffen moaned, taking a big mouthful of Amadeo's testicle. Steffen hummed with delight, the sounds of satisfaction vibrating through Amadeo's balls and down his dong.

"Jack me, you slave!" Amadeo now ordered. "Spank that ass harder, Mistress Willow!"

Between each whipping, Willow would rub her palm over the affected area. Instead of shriveling at the beating, Steffen's prick stood out proudly, shiny and purple. It would jump every time Willow would spank it, and Steffen would flinch slightly, but it would increase the passion with which he suckled Amadeo's balls or jacked his dick. Amadeo knew there was power in submission. Steffen could look like the most submissive bottom in the world while sucking Amadeo's dick and having his balls slapped by a fully-clad lady, but Steffen really did control the situation. He could, of course, stop at any time and no one would prevent him. But his submission was massively turning Amadeo on, and it really seemed to be riling Willow as well. She gyrated her pubic mound against his gorgeous ass, pinched his nipples, and had the good fortune to run her palms across those well-developed pecs.

Amadeo had an idea. "Satisfy him, Mistress. Get down below him on your shoulders and suck that big schlong you've been whipping. Look how hard and purple it is. You've got him so worked up he'll flood your mouth in seconds."

Willow cooed, "I don't think I can take this big cock in my mouth."

Amadeo agreed. "It's not easy swallowing that big tool, but it's fun trying. Make a daisy chain."

Steffen sucked on Amadeo's bursting glans as though it were candy. When he tickled the slit with his tongue-tip Amadeo gasped, and had to push the man to back off. Steffen said, "A daisy chain would mean you were licking Willow's pussy. That pussy's mine, buddy."

"But we're just doing this to please Willow. Right, Willow? Would you like me to lick your pretty little pussy?"

Willow had already eagerly positioned herself beneath Steffen, the mop flogger tossed aside. His hanging ball sac swayed right in her face and already she had gripped his massive tool and was mouthing it. “I don’t want to offend my sweet Steffen.”

“Damn straight,” said Steffen, looking down at Willow with what could only be called love. “No other guy gets his mouth near that pussy. *Oh, good Lord!*”

Willow had swallowed as much of Steffen’s big prick as she could, hoovering up and down on the well-hung cock. When Steffen fucked her mouth, the sexy undulating sway of his lower back and ass drove Amadeo over the edge. “Eat me, you fucking slave!” Amadeo cried, because he knew he was already coming. He came so fast and copiously Steffen struggled to eat it all, but it was bad form to spit any out if you hoped to suck that person again. And Steffen apparently had been around the Racquet Club often enough—had his cock sucked by other ladies, no doubt—to know that as well. He gulped admirably, but Amadeo could feel some of it dribble from the corner of the cocksucker’s mouth. He felt for him, he really did, especially since Steffen was apparently now spewing his own load into his girlfriend’s mouth. She would have quite a job to keep up with that.

When Amadeo’s spasms subsided and he stopped choking on his own cries, he reluctantly allowed Steffen to disengage and focus on his own orgasm. Amadeo sat back on the spanking bench where Willow had been getting herself off to watch Steffen flood her mouth with his jism. She couldn’t take it all—it looked as though some adorably came out her nose—and watching the fluid gyrations of Steffen’s hips and ass as he lewdly fucked her mouth had Amadeo wondering if he could, after all, get it up so soon again after coming.

He had a new goal in life now. He wanted to fuck Steffen’s delicious ass.

Chapter Seven

What was that Steffen had called her? "Sublime." Willow felt sublime sucking his cock.

Steffen carefully held his hips above her, angling his cock into her mouth just shy of choking her. He had obviously done this before, pinned a woman—or a *man?*—to the floor to fuck her mouth. He was a skilled operator. He must have sucked many cocks, too, in his time. She could watch in the mirror as he accepted Amadeo's load, and he gulped every drop. It was ten times more erotic than her fuzzy remembering of the Daytona Beach college experience. Now she worried, though, as she pistoned his hefty meat in and out of her mouth. Just how experienced *was* Steffen in the world of butt pirates? She mentioned an obscure fantasy to him one day, and the next day they were acting it out—with a fellow Steffen had apparently known when he was a quarterback!

Steffen's bulging, velvety glans massaged her upper palate. She wasn't choking at all, surprisingly for the size of his massive tool. But she wasn't prepared for the sheer volume of his load. Willow had sucked Matt, of course, and a few men before him, naturally. And watching these two virile men fondling and making love to each other had made her so juicy she was wide open with lust. Someone could have slid a rococo bedpost inside of her and she wouldn't have noticed, she was that hot and bothered.

But the men were taunting her, teasing her with their own orgasms. Amadeo now leaned back on the spanking bench, arms crossed, displaying his absolutely stunning pecs, watching with amusement as Willow struggled to swallow Steffen's load. His semen tasted surprisingly wonderful, as though he'd been eating fruit, sweet and fresh. But some trickled from the corners of her mouth and she couldn't contain it all manfully, as Steffen had when eating Amadeo's load as if it were nectar of the gods.

Steffen's entire body stiffened as he came, a thorough shudder running up and down his entire body. What a slut she was, and she loved it! Her sluttiest moment to date had been doing it with Matt in a gas station restroom—with the door locked. Matt had nothing on these two delicious, randy studs, one of whom was now pumping her throat full of his seed. She felt all-powerful and free, knowing she could drive not one but *two* men to such randy heights.

"Whew." Willow wiped her mouth with the back of her hand as Steffen collapsed back on his hands. Amadeo bounced off the spanking bench to put his hands under her arms and help her stand. All she had to do was smooth down her dress. She had worn the little black dress in the hopes it would impress Steffen. It seemed to have worked. "So," she said, chipper, looking down at the sprawled, half-naked man. "Are you going to lift Mr. Barbieri's stop work order?"

Willow loved that crooked grin. "That would be corruption. If I lifted it for you, I'd have to lift it for every guy who sucks my dick."

"Right," agreed Amadeo. "The way it is now, every permit applicant just sucks your cock for free."

The men laughed, but it raised an insecurity in Willow. Her husband had withdrawn from her and sought comfort in the arms of other women. *She wanted Steffen.* She would tolerate no fooling around from this man. She had to think of a casual way to phrase her question. "Seriously, Steffen. Do you do that often—fool around with men on the jobs?"

"Yeah," agreed Amadeo. "I had the same question. You just showed absolutely no resistance when I popped your cock into my mouth. You'd obviously done it before."

"You're a fine one to talk." Steffen didn't even bother stuffing his big prick back into his jeans. Even flaccid, the enormous appendage lay across his hip, pulsing with a life of its own. “Mr. Racquet Club. But to answer your question, Willow, no. When Amadeo, ah, propositioned me yesterday, my response was to punch him. Then I thought of your fantasy. I thought I’d do anything to make it come true. You’re a sublime beauty, Willow. I don’t know why you’re alone—it’s none of my business—but it seems a shame.”

“Amen to that, bro,” said Amadeo.

“Having to date guys who bring their own jet packs and flasks of booze on dates with women.”

“What?” scoffed Amadeo.

Steffen continued, “You deserve better than that. Hell, you deserve *me*. Which is why I was willing to give it a shot with this cowboy.”

“Such a sacrifice,” Willow acknowledged. “Well, *look* at him, Steffen! He’s banging hot. Do you run into a lot of hunks like this in your inspection business?”

“Not many,” Steffen admitted, finally getting to his feet and arranging his cock and balls. “I just now realized I knew this one from Twelve Palms High School.”

“He was a jock, too? He said you were the quarterback.” She hated feeling shallow, but frankly, it thrilled Willow knowing she’d just sucked a quarterback’s cock. She had been a dumpy mathlete in her Florida high school. She had only blossomed in her early twenties when she’d finally lost a bit of weight, grown tits, and gotten work as a secretary at a door company. Matt used to hang doors before he got into the house flipping business with his dad.

Steffen said, “No, if I recall correctly, Amadeo, you sort of hung around with the stoner crowd, didn’t you?”

“That was me,” Amadeo said proudly. “Played a Les Paul in that famous garage band, The Unbearable Rightness of Swing.”

“He wasn’t nearly this buff,” Steffen told Willow. “He sort of slouched around with long greasy hair, thinking he was so cool.”

"Weren't we?" Amadeo protested. "I mean, come now. Those plaid, tattered shirts were the epitome of cool, listening to Soundgarden and Nine Inch Nails. My *father* didn't think so, but..."

While amusing, none of this answered Willow's question. She faced Steffen squarely, head on. "So tell me. Do you consider yourself bisexual? Have you had boyfriends in the past?"

Amadeo chuckled. "You make it sound as though it's a disgusting crime. For what it's worth, I've been playing with boys and girls my entire life. I'm equal opportunity."

Willow felt ashamed. Amadeo was right. She *had* made it sound low and undesirable. "What I mean to say is, there's nothing wrong with it. You just seem like such a *natural* with Amadeo."

Steffen chuckled, too. He seemed proud of his performance. "I'm a complete and utter noob, Willow. Never even kissed another man. We don't have to repeat it again if you've got your kink out of your system."

"Hey," protested Amadeo.

Willow put soothing palms on Steffen's chest. "No, no, not at all. I doubt that specific kink will *ever* be out of my system, Steffen. You and Amadeo make a compatible couple, I think. And somehow I don't think you were faking that passion and eagerness for his cock, Steffen."

Steffen reddened and looked aside, still grinning. "It was...nice. Different. I'm not going to be close-minded and say I didn't like it."

"Hey, check this out," said Amadeo. From a matching nightstand next to the elaborate rococo bed he had taken a silk-inlaid box. Willow went to peek around his arm. In the box were two gold-plated balls, about one inch in diameter.

"So? What are they?"

Steffen peeked around Amadeo's shoulder too. "What else has ole Cesar Romero been up to?"

Willow reminded him, "We don't *really* know this was Cesar Romero's room. I just picked a name out of a hat. For all we know, this room *could* have been Norman Fell's."

"Oh, yeah?" Amadeo snorted. "Well, then ole Norman Fell forgot to take his Ben Wa balls when they abandoned this motel."

"Or Swifty Lazar," said Steffen, taking the box. "Or Neutra, or Cody, or Lautner."

Willow knew he recited the names of some architects he revered. "What do the balls do?"

Amadeo explained, "You insert them inside a woman, and she walks around all day with them. Supposed to tone the muscles, sort of like doing kegel exercises."

"*Well!*" said Willow, pretending to be insulted. "I hardly need kegel exercises. I've never even had a child—" She stopped suddenly and looked at both men. She mentally begged them to change the subject.

Steffen seemed to pick up on her plea. He shook the box with the balls. "Hm. These don't contain chimes. You could easily walk around with them in—shall we try?"

His look was so devilish, how could she say no? "So it just increases my muscle strength, because I have to concentrate on keeping them in?"

Amadeo said, "And rolling them around. Allegedly it's a subtle turn-on. Here, let me wash them. Do you have running water?"

"Yes, Cesar's sink should work."

"There's even some bar soap in here," Amadeo called. "Looks like it could be about forty years old, for sure."

"Whatever works," Steffen called back. With shining eyes, already he had bent at the knees to hitch his thumbs under the shred of fabric that was Willow's panties.

It was the ultimate in forbidden, locking gazes with the studly inspector who was sliding her panties from her. She stepped out of them—luckily he dropped them on the new carpet without seeming to notice that they were absolutely soaked with her juices.

But he didn't stop there. He drew her to him, sliding one hot palm up the slope of her ass, around the curve of it, cupping it. Now her ass and thunder thighs were bared to several of the damning mirrors. She squirmed uncomfortably, but she knew this moment would come sooner or later. She just had to hope Steffen wasn't an aficionado of the "Low-Fat Delights" other women had to offer.

"Lovely, just lovely," Steffen whispered.

Amadeo was coming out of the bathroom. "Okay, these washed up just fine, look like they've never been—*whoa*. Nice view." He seemed to admire Willow's bare ass, which oddly made her even more self-aware. "I presume it's your turn to insert these balls."

"I'm doing all of the ball-inserting around here," said Steffen. He didn't take his eyes off Willow to hold a hand out to accept the balls.

Amadeo put his hands on his hops. "Now, how's this going to work, may I ask? You're the only one who gets to pet her pussy. You're the only one who gets to insert any balls. What do I get to do?"

Willow didn't want to alienate the hulking cowboy. She had never seen a more erotic sight than watching Steffen on his knees servicing the strapping caveman, and she sure as hell didn't want it to stop when it was just getting started. The two men had chemistry together in more ways than one. "Oh, dear Amadeo," she said plaintively, "I think Steffen just wants a chance to try me out first. Am I wrong, dear Steffen? *Ah!*"

"Damn straight. Ah. Your pussy is wet as can be."

Steffen's fingertips tickled the edges of her labia, staying just this close from her hot button. Willow sucked in air through her teeth and shivered on her tiptoes. She noticed she was clutching poor Steffen's shoulders so tightly she could have drawn blood.

But his murmur was cool, collected. "What got you so hot, my little minx? Was it maybe watching me slide this other man's prick down my throat?"

Willow shimmied her hips from side to side, hoping to catch his fingertip on her clit. "Maybe," she admitted, suddenly shy.

"You're as wet as a fisherman's slipper."

Ah. There. Godammit. Willow hissed in air when his finger brushed her quivering clit.

Amadeo took exception to Steffen's words. "That's not a pretty picture, Steffen. How's about she's as wet as a swordfish."

Willow felt one of the balls pop inside her pussy. They weren't very big, and she wondered how they would stay inside her. Maybe that was the secret—she would have to keep flexing those muscles or a ball would roll out onto the floor in the middle of trying to talk to a contractor.

Pressing his torso to her from behind, Amadeo slid his hands up to support her breasts. The shirred bodice didn't do much to cradle their weight, and immediately Amadeo was pinching her nipples, sending more electrical shocks darting into her pussy, centering on her clit. She was surprised that Steffen "allowed" Amadeo to fondle her tits, but he was occupied elsewhere.

The balls were connected by a string, and Steffen inserted the second one. Now he diddled at her clitoris more vigorously, and his intent was plain. *Bastard. He's going to make me come. I'll be completely dependent on him if I want to come again. Like Pavlov's dogs. I'll keep coming back for more. I'll get wet when just thinking about him and his talented—*

"Oh God, oh God, oh God!" Willow heard someone crying out, surprised to discover it was herself. Amadeo had slid the spaghetti straps of her slinky dress down, baring her tits for both men to see. When he pinched her bare nipples the sudden stimulation sent arrows right through her clit. Between Amadeo's tweaking and Steffen's diddling her slippery clit, she was instantly on the verge of orgasm.

"That's right," Steffen encouraged her. "Take your time. Fall right into it. We're here to catch you. Good girl. Let Amadeo play with your nipples. Take a bite, Amadeo. Her tits are so luscious and full and—"

One enormous flutter of her entire canal, and Willow's pelvis was wrenched with a blissful spasm. When Amadeo's teeth clamped around her right nipple, everything crashed in around her. Wave after exquisite wave rolled through her cunt, gripping her uterus with a powerful hand. She knew she was shaking and shuddering like a fool, but Steffen encouraged it.

"Good. Good girl. Let it come. Come for us, baby. Come for us."

It seemed to go on forever, Amadeo's teeth nibbling away, Steffen twiddling her clit, slower and slower as the contractions ebbed. Willow came to, finding herself twitching and gulping air like a child trying to hold in a sob. Gasping, she pressed on Amadeo's forehead, forcibly removing him from her tit. It was too much. Too, too much!

The men even chuckled as she detached herself! She smoothed down her dress and replaced her tit in the bodice. "Enough already!" she protested. She shimmied her hips to ensure the Ben Wa balls were still inside her canal. "Gads! You two men are going to be the death of me!"

She tried to stalk with dignity into Cesar's bathroom, but Amadeo was laughing. "Good thing those aren't the kind of balls that jingle."

Steffen was laughing, too. "I wonder what the purpose of the chimes is."

"I guess so you can hear the gal coming," suggested Amadeo. "Like a cat scaring away the birds."

Willow slammed the bathroom door. *Good riddance! Men. So arrogant. So full of themselves. So certain of their own success.*

However, she couldn't deny that the men had succeeded. She was hopelessly smitten with both of them. Steffen had been right—Amadeo *was* her "type." How did Steffen already know her type? He seemed to already know her so well it was frightening.

She had to get back to the contractor surfacing her swimming pool, but she recalled many items she had wanted to discuss with the men. The two men who had just given her the biggest, most outrageous orgasm of her life.

"Hey, guys," she said as she exited the bathroom. "We need to start moving this equipment into the—oh, hello."

A worker was standing in Cesar's room eyeballing the spanking bench. She recognized the guy as a laborer for Chas White, the amazing vanishing contractor. She needed to speak to Chas, and apparently Amadeo did, too, because he was now telling the worker,

"Tell Chas to call Amadeo Barbieri over at the Lone Palm Ranch. Tell him the building inspector put a stop work order on my tack room and I'm not pleased with his work."

"No shit," the African-American worker agreed. "I've worked for Chas for two years and have seen him maybe a handful of times. I hate to say that about a boss of mine, but it's the truth. He's as rare as a sincere fart in church."

"Where does he go the whole day?" Willow asked.

"Well, it's a matter of great speculation among us workers. I really shouldn't speculate in front of clients, but he does leave us holding the bag most of the time. Let's just say, he's an aficionado of *tennis*."

Willow didn't understand, but her two men seemed to. "*Ah*," said Amadeo knowingly. "All right, then. Thanks, Carl. I can probably find him over at the Racquet Club myself."

Carl turned to leave. He pointed back over his shoulder. "And he probably likes that bench, too."

Willow said, "Tell him to call Willow Paige, too! Well, that was weird. Listen, guys. I was trying to tell you about Ronnie Dobbs way back when I first came in. I talked to Jaclyn's boyfriend, Fernando."

"I'm familiar with him," said Steffen. "He does a lot of work around town."

"He does?" Willow was surprised that Fernando was actually known for work. "Anyway, Ronnie Dobbs is currently incarcerated at the county jail. He was arrested playing air guitar on the arm of that giant T. Rex statue alongside the highway, so he won't be harassing me for a few days at least."

Steffen nodded. "He has a Beaumont address, so he was probably on his way back home when he got arrested. He was just playing air guitar? Doesn't sound like much of a reason to arrest a guy, even The Most Arrested Man in the Coachella Valley. I'm going to put a BOLO out on his truck, make sure he gets stopped if he's anywhere within a ten-mile radius of the Searchlight Motel."

Willow said, "Well, obviously the air guitar wasn't the whole thing. Apparently Ronnie tried to run from the cops who were yelling at him from one of those megaphones. But he fell down and started flailing around, so the cops easily arrested him."

Amadeo chuckled. "Sounds like a major character."

"Oh, he *is*," Steffen assured him. "He came sniffing around here looking for some artifact, but he was so creepy I scared him off. Why was he flailing around, did they figure out?"

"Well," said Willow. "Apparently he'd been snorting some fire ants to celebrate some *Wizard of Oz* thing. The ants bit his trachea and it swelled up, so he had trouble breathing. Then he claimed police brutality."

"Oh, he always does that," said Steffen. "You should see his police record. In between the arrests, it's one long incident of 'police brutality.' I wonder what *The Wizard of Oz* has to do with fire ants."

Amadeo helped out. "Let me guess. It wasn't *The Wizard of Oz*. Was it Ozzfest?"

Willow clapped her hands together. "*That* was it! Ozzfest! How'd you know? What *is* Ozzfest?"

Amadeo said, "There's an urban legend that Ozzy Osbourne—he's some heavy metal guy—snorted fire ants. What a moron.

Everyone knows you can't snort fire ants. They haven't held an Ozzfest since 2010."

"Says the guy who knows." Steffen chided him good-naturedly. "Must be your experience in the Unbearable Rightness of Swing."

Willow giggled. "Well, Ronnie is off the streets for awhile anyway. I don't think we have anything to fear from him. He's just a high goofball."

"And wife-beater," Steffen told Amadeo.

"What?" Amadeo puffed up to greater proportions when angry. "Let's get this BOLO out on this guy, Steffen. I've got more than a few friends down at County."

"Same here," said Steffen. "Let's go down in person, if we can't find Chas White first. Listen, Willow, my little sunset palomino." His reference to her motel's former business reminded Willow that she hadn't told Steffen about the "menu" she had found. But he seemed in a rush to depart with Amadeo. "Keep those balls in, my little filly. We'll be back tonight to take you to dinner. Right, Amadeo?"

"But of course," agreed Amadeo.

Willow liked being a "little filly" so much she didn't mind when the men left for the County. She dove back into her remodeling work with gusto. She was reminded with every step that she took of the two men who had given her the gift of the amazing orgasm. For some reason they seemed as though they wanted to date her—seriously date her. It had been so long since she had noticed anyone make a pass at her, Willow was entirely skeptical. But the two balls rolling against each other inside of her told her otherwise.

Chapter Eight

"I actually admire it."

Steffen turned to Amadeo. He was pleasantly surprised to hear the rancher utter such a sentiment about the house that seemed made mostly of wall-to-ceiling glass wrapped around a few giant boulders. Horizontal planes resting upon horizontal planes seemed suspended in space over the invisible walls. The Kupka Desert House was probably Steffen's favorite example of Desert Modern in the entire valley, designed by his idol, Neutra. Outdoor rooms were protected from desert sandstorms by vertical windscreens that could be moved about. Just like in Willow's Searchlight Motel, breezeways connected wings. It was probably the most famous private residence in the valley, but the trio had to view it from a nearby bluff at the foot of Mount San Jacinto. There were no tours.

Steffen said, "But you've lived here your whole life and told me you never admired this style."

Amadeo tilted his head thoughtfully. "I think when you're used to seeing a certain thing, you wind up not appreciating it much."

"Take it for granted," added Willow. "Like I take the Everglades for granted because that's all I ever knew. I came out here and was so stunned by the beauty of the desert. I always thought it was one empty expanse, but there's so much to see."

This was their second official date. Two nights ago the three had done the dinner and dancing thing in Palm Springs. They hadn't seen each other yesterday due to some building inspecting, ranching, and remodeling business, and it was just hell on Steffen. He realized how quickly he had bonded with both of the others. Of course it was

Willow who entranced him, but Steffen was shocked to realize he missed Amadeo, too, that entire endlessly long day he spent without them.

He had started his alternately dominant/submissive relationship with the buff rancher as a tease to lure in Willow. He knew it would turn Willow on to watch the two men making love to each other. He had been correct about that—and then some—but what surprised Steffen the most was how well they all got along without making love. They had dined and danced the night away without so much as a hot kiss between each other, so Steffen knew it wasn't just a flash in the pan fling. The men had dropped Willow off at the Searchlight Motel after dancing and had gone their separate ways.

All day yesterday, inspecting electrical upgrades and checking site plans, Steffen had been distracted by thoughts of Amadeo as well as Willow. What was going on? Amadeo was supposed to be a lure, a toy, a tease. Steffen had never entertained lusty thoughts about another man. Suddenly he found himself reminiscing about the tasty blow job he had given the strapping cowboy—not just the one he'd received. At the hetero dance club they had taken turns giving Willow spins around the floor, but Steffen had spent almost as much time admiring Amadeo's ass as Willow's.

"Oh, the desert is fascinating," Steffen agreed with Willow. "When my dad told me we were moving here from Ireland, I was all about rebelling. Kicking walls, yelling, protesting. To go from the rolling green hills to the…well, the flat empty expanse of desert was the biggest injustice, I thought."

"Didn't stop you from becoming the quarterback," Amadeo groused.

Steffen grinned. He would never stop lording it over Amadeo about having been on the football team while Amadeo slunk around being alienated and angst-filled. Especially since now Amadeo had bloomed into such a powerful, dominant rancher, it was one of the only areas where Steffen *could* lord it over him. "Wait until you're here in the spring, Willow. Of course first you notice the California fan palms. But even now in June, look at the grass and scrub."

"I can vouch for that," said Amadeo. He had to ride through it every day.

Steffen continued. "And these ocotillo. Or look at that group of palms, growing right out of that solid rock."

Today they had toured the iconic space-age gas station and Elvis's Honeymoon Hideaway and driven through the Twin Palms Estates of mid-century tract houses. Now in the early evening hours they were getting as close to the famed Kupka House as possible. As a board member of the Palm Springs Modern Committee, Steffen had been lucky enough to have been inside the house several times, but not today. They had to walk around the perimeter and view what they could of the glass pavilion, the pinwheel design of the famous house.

Steffen said like a tour guide, "See that corner of the house? Those palms were already growing out of those rocks, so they built around it."

Willow hiked up the bluff a bit to get a better view, the two men trailing her. Amadeo asked Steffen, "So you rebelled against your dad?"

"Oh, not too heavily. We got along fairly well until he died of cancer five years ago. It was just the usual teenaged insubordination. I used to deal with your dad when I'd go out to inspect stuff on your ranch. How's he doing?"

Amadeo snorted. "Dying of cancer."

Steffen frowned. "You don't seem too…"

"Sensitive about it? I'm not." They had reached where Willow stood, and she looked at them with mild curiosity. Amadeo crossed his arms in front of his barrel chest. Steffen now knew he did that when he wanted to regain some feeling of authority or control. Amadeo looked out at the desert. "My father was an asshole. You probably didn't notice that part of him."

Oh, Steffen had noticed it all right. Salvatore Barbieri was an irascible old coot, constantly bitching and challenging Steffen's observations. Salvatore had always done things up to building code, in his own mind. Steffen was always wrong—Mr. Barbieri was always right. "I did get that impression, yeah."

"So when I turned eighteen I left the ranch. I moved into the city where I lived a sort of dissipated life and—don't laugh—worked in a music store."

Willow laughed anyway. At least she covered her mouth. "I'm sorry. I just can't see you with long hair, being a grunge hippie."

Amadeo smiled good-naturedly. "But I was. I just lived a party lifestyle throughout my twenties, rebelling against my father's iron-fisted command. I started experimenting with men just to rebel but found out I liked it. I've probably been bi my entire life."

Willow took Amadeo's arm and held it close to her bosom. "Well, I'm certainly glad. It's working out perfectly for us. How did you come to inherit the ranch, then?"

"Well, that was a strange situation. When I was thirty—eight years ago—it became obvious my dad couldn't manage the ranch anymore. So he finally sends someone to find me, after not having contacted me in ten years. Suddenly when he needed a ranch manager, someone to carry on in his name, I was needed. So spitefully, I told him I had a bunch of boyfriends. Jee-zus. Near about gave him a heart attack on top of his cancer, now that I look back on it. You know how arrogant and selfish twenty-somethings can be."

"And thirty-somethings. Crap," Willow said in commiseration. She stroked Amadeo's admirable, hairless chest. He wore only a tight wifebeater T-shirt, but his olive Italian skin could take the heat. Steffen had to cover up with a button-down shirt. "So how did you wind up with the ranch? He's still alive, right?"

"Well, eventually he called me back into his hospital room. He said he still wasn't cool with all my nancy-boy shenanigans but he figured I'd get over it eventually, it was just a phase. I tried telling him I was never 'getting over it' because I actually *liked* it, but by that time the lawyer was already handing me the deed to the ranch, so to speak. See, there was one tiny detail my father couldn't overlook. I'm the only son."

"*Ah*," said Steffen. He'd had to deal with a lot of property ownership issues in his career. It was interesting how men from the old country could suddenly easily overlook major "transgressions" if a man was his only son. That trumped all sorts of perversions, apparently. "It's the Italian thing."

"Exactly," said Amadeo. "He'd rather give the ranch to a twisted, deviant son than his daughter who is a married flight attendant with two kids."

Steffen said, "Well, with all due respect, I'd have to say you deserved the ranch. You're doing a great job from what I can see, aside from the Chas White-built tack room."

"Yes," agreed Willow, although she'd never seen Amadeo's ranch. She took his chin in her fingers and forced him to look her in the eyes. He was over a foot taller than her, and they looked like a fairy tale couple. "Amadeo, you're doing a fantastic job. You must understand. Your father is old school. He is never going to accept that you're bisexual."

"Thank—"

Willow cut off Amadeo's gratitude with a kiss. Steffen simmered and cleared his throat nearby, expecting it to finish soon. The couple had never kissed, that Steffen knew of, and already jealousy bit at the inside of his stomach. But that backstabber Amadeo deepened the kiss, taking Willow's fragile chin in his big paw and closing his bearish, sensual mouth over her little pouty one.

Steffen waited as it became evident Amadeo was licking Willow's tongue. Steffen got behind Willow and slid his hands around her ribcage to cup her ample tits. It seemed she had been getting more comfortable in her own skin in front of the men, because today she wore a strappy dress with push-up brassiere cups. Her tits jiggled when she walked, and Steffen was glad they were only playing tourist, and not in a nightclub where other men might ogle her.

Amadeo encircled her waist with his giant hands. It was obvious the two men were fighting, literally, for the upper hand. Steffen put a palm against Amadeo's bare shoulder and shoved. "All right. Enough." The couple parted with a hungry, smacking sound.

Willow turned to look innocently at Steffen. "What's wrong, sweetie? You're not jealous that Amadeo kisses me, are you? I thought we were all equal."

Amadeo answered for him. "He's not jealous. He just wants you to himself—to do more with you. Here, sit on this rock in the shade." Amadeo wasn't being entirely truthful, but it smoothed over the awkward moment very diplomatically.

Amadeo successfully distracted Willow as he seated her on a low, flat rock hidden from the setting sun by a boulder. As the sun fell behind the mountains, someone inside the Kupka House turned on a few lights. The immaculate turquoise swimming pool was lit from within, too. Steffen wanted to enjoy his meaningful feeling of a bond with the architect Neutra, but Willow posed on the rock was more attractive. Steffen fell to his knees before her.

"My little filly," he said. He had seen some gangster call a gal that on an old movie, and it fit with the whole Palomino Ranch motif of her motel. Steffen knew women couldn't resist his German-Irish accent, and Willow was no exception. Was it wrong to use this to his advantage? *Why the hell not?* He petted her face with the back of his hand. "It does make me jealous to see Amadeo kiss you, but I'll get over it, I hope. I just want to be the only one pleasuring you. What if Amadeo is better at it than me? You see my dilemma."

"Sweetie," cooed Willow. "What do you have to be worried about? You're the sexiest, tastiest man I've ever met. You were obviously so skilled the other day at giving me a hand relief party."

Steffen was perplexed. "A…a *what?*"

Willow grinned secretively. She reached into her giant handbag that she'd thrown onto the ground by the rock. Amadeo kneeled beside Steffen to see what Willow pulled from the bag. It was a piece of shiny black cardboard that declared in pink lettering:

The Best Fillies in California!
Ranch Delights

"What the fuck?" said Steffen, taking the cardboard from Willow's fingers.

"It's a menu I found in an old file drawer in the motel office."

A slow smile spread over Steffen's face. Apparently Willow had discovered a bill of fare from the old "World Famous" Sunset Palomino Ranch. "This is a great find, Willow! Look at this. A Hand Relief Party is one of the appetizers."

Amadeo said, "I guess we're just getting started. Hey, look. Bondage Dungeon. That must've been the room we were in the other day."

"No doubt," said Steffen, eagerly scanning the offerings. "Some of these are obvious, but others are kind of obscure. Like, what's a Milky Way?"

Amadeo said right off the bat, "That's when men like to nuzzle women who are lactating." His hand automatically shot out to fondle one of Willow's breasts, although he didn't take his eyes from the menu.

Steffen's hand automatically shot out to slap Amadeo's hand away. "Okay, you're the expert."

"The sexpert." Willow giggled.

"Then what's this? A Spit Roast? I can picture a pig on a spit being roasted over a barbecue. That doesn't conjure up anything particularly sexy."

"That's easy," said Amadeo. "That can be combined with a Feast at the Y."

Steffen scoffed. "I can figure out what *that* is."

"Oh yeah?" Amadeo's tone was challenging. "Then *do* it, lover boy." To assist, Amadeo took Willow's skirt hem between his fingers and slid it up her thigh.

Willow didn't protest, but cast Steffen a low, sultry look. "It *is* on the entrée menu, Steffen." She parted her thighs to indicate her willingness to give Steffen a Feast at the Y. She leaned back on the rock on one hand and hitched one sandal up into a cranny, giving Steffen a display of her narrow thong, her pussy lips bulging enticingly on either side of the fabric strip.

Amadeo moved behind Steffen, rubbing the back of his neck with encouragement. "Go ahead, bro. Have your fill."

Steffen needed no more enticing. He considered himself a proficient muff diver. That Domme he had lived with had often "queened" him while he was tied up, so he had developed strong throat and tongue muscles. That was a couple of years ago, though—he'd been a swinging bachelor ever since, and bachelors didn't often run around performing cunnilingus. Still, Steffen calculated in his head as he dove in to take tiny, licking bites of Willow's inner thighs. It had taken her approximately thirty seconds to come the other day when he'd given her that Hand Relief Party. And she still had the Ben Wa balls inside of her. This wouldn't take long at all.

He hadn't counted, though, on being so utterly distracted by Amadeo.

First off, Amadeo reached around and grabbed one of Steffen's wrists. Before Steffen could protest—if he had wanted to—he was once again cuffed, this time with his wrists in front of him. He tried not to miss a beat in his tonguing of Willow. Her inner thigh was like a creamy pillow, and she twitched every time he licked her. He hooked a finger around the strip of fabric and pulled it aside. When he touched the tip of his nose to the clitoris that peeked from between her labia, she gasped.

"*Oh! Steffen!*"

That was a good sign, and she clutched the back of his skull to cradle him to her.

But Amadeo couldn't just let him have his fun. He cupped Steffen's stiff penis, clothed inside his jeans, and squeezed. "This is all I imagined after seeing you in the shower at school. I'd cuff you to the shower head and suck on this long, fat cock."

"That's right," Willow encouraged. Steffen didn't know if the spoke to him or Amadeo, but either was fine. "That's perfect."

Steffen reached out his tongue-tip to swipe at the bulging clitoris, and Willow near about tore a handful of his hair out. He was doing it right, this Feast at the Y.

Amadeo's other hand unbuckled Steffen's belt while he massaged his lover's erection. "After seeing this long, fat hose on you, it was all I could think of. You were soaping your crotch, squeezing your ball sac, wringing soap from your long tool, and I know I wasn't the only one letching after you with desire. Some of your fellow teammates gazed a bit too long at your dick. More than one guy had a hard-on after watching you shower."

By the time Amadeo released Steffen's cock into the air, Steffen was on fire. Amadeo's praise was pumping up more than his ego. The image of being desired by a locker room full of stiff football players was exciting him. Willow gyrated her hips as she propped herself up on the rock, assisting Steffen to find that sweet spot she seemed to favor. He had fingered her on this exact spot the other day when she'd gone off like a rocket, and he found it again with his tongue, flicking it across the spot rapidly.

"*Oh! Good God!* Don't stop!" Willow panted like a steam engine, her voice getting increasingly higher with each note.

Steffen did miss a beat, however, when Amadeo gripped his dick and squeezed. Steffen nearly lost it. Amadeo curved his buff torso over Steffen's back and gave his cock a few good pumps.

Amadeo murmured in his ear. "Be prepared for the pounding of your life."

Chapter Nine

Amadeo was driven nearly insane with lust. He finally had what he wanted—the studly quarterback's big prick in his hand. Handcuffed, and with ass bared to him. Helpless. This was how he'd imagined Steffen in his wildest dreams for two decades now. And he finally had him. It was a turn-on, too, to watch Steffen muff-diving with such enthusiasm.

Once Willow saw what Amadeo was up to, she couldn't seem to take her limpid eyes from Amadeo. She gyrated her hips while fondling Steffen's head, but she avidly watched as Amadeo fisted her boyfriend's cock and talked nasty.

"Get ready for me to use you, you fucking stud," Amadeo growled. He tore off his own wifebeater T-shirt to give Willow something else to admire. Spitting into his hand, he applied his palm to the exposed asshole, fingering the puckered entrance, tickling it. Steffen reflexively clenched his cheeks but admirably didn't neglect Willow for more than a split second. Her eyes grew rounder and her mouth went slacker as Amadeo unsheathed his own tool and rubbed the bulging glans against the delicious opening. He, too, gripped the back of Steffen's neck, and he had to let go of Steffen's cock in order to slick up his own.

"Use him, Amadeo," Willow encouraged. She looked lopsided, deranged with passion. "Give him a good fucking. Ride him like a pony. Roast him on your spit."

When Amadeo made the first tentative, slight push against his anus, Steffen withdrew from Willow's steamy pussy. "Amadeo," he panted, "I've never been used that way. A dildo, maybe. But no guy has ever—"

"Silence," Amadeo commanded, "or I'll have to put a bit in your mouth too."

Their nasty talk must have distracted Steffen well enough, for when Amadeo broached the tight ring and penetrated the chiseled quarterback, Steffen just tossed his head back and moaned silently. Willow allowed him a break, as she appeared fascinated with the way Amadeo corkscrewed his hips professionally, sinking himself a little deeper inside Steffen every time. Now Amadeo was free to handle Steffen's cock again, but he was careful not to bring him off too rapidly. Timing was of the essence in a spit roast. He kneaded the stiff dick lightly, enjoying the slick feel of the shaft in his fist.

"That's good," he murmured approvingly. His hand on the back of Steffen's neck directed his face back into Willow's pussy, and she purred with delight. "You're going to like this. You're going to be begging for more, wait and see. Not a man on this planet who doesn't like being fucked up the ass, especially by a cowboy like me. *Ah.* There. There you go." His cockhead hit Steffen's prostate gland, and he could actually feel the immense shudder that rolled down Steffen's spine. Steffen's dick pulsed in his hand as the seed surged up the length of it, and again, Steffen rolled his head back on a rubbery neck.

When Steffen's rectum began to clutch at Amadeo's cock, he lost it, too. "That's it," Amadeo choked. Only half his brain was trying to shove Steffen's face back into Willow's pretty bush. The other half was swept away on a tidal wave of ecstasy. His dick pulsed deep inside the heated depths of his lover, while Steffen's seed flowed over his wrist. "Eat her," Amadeo barely managed to say. He felt like a crow on an electric fence the way he was twitching and jerking, buried inside the man he'd wanted so long.

He didn't know how Steffen maintained it—some men could walk and chew gum at the same time, and some, like Amadeo, couldn't—

but he lapped away at Willow's juicy pussy like a pro. She kept up a steady chatter, only some of which made sense.

"Oh, God! That's good. Don't stop. Steffen. Don't stop. *Oh, God! You hit it right. That's it. Eat…my…Y!"*

That last got to Amadeo, and he recovered somewhat from his shuddering coma in time to chuckle. Willow certainly was a talker, and a funny one at that. He got the feeling she had some pain in her recent past. There was that ex-husband in Florida she seemed to be running from, emotionally. Well, who hadn't wished they were an entire continent away from their ex on occasion? Amadeo stumbled behind the boulder to freshen up and find where he'd flung his T-shirt.

He had to chuckle again when he saw Steffen attempting to pull away from his feast. Willow twitched like a worm at the end of a hook, manipulating Steffen's head with a handful of his hair. "I'm still coming!" she hiccupped. She alternately pushed and pulled Steffen's head toward her pelvis, seemingly unsure whether she wanted to continue or not. Finally she squealed like a teapot going off and shoved Steffen away. He sat there with a witless grin, wiping his face with the back of his hand.

Amadeo helped him to his feet, and they wandered down the slope to admire the Kupka House lit up like a spaceship. "Now that I know you, I can see this architecture differently. I did always take it for granted."

"Your ranch house has a mid-century desert flavor to it," said Steffen. "Your kitchen has those hanging globe lamps, that mod wet bar, and if I recall correctly, some period David Smock furnishings."

"David Smock? I wouldn't know David Smock from Spock. You mean I could be sitting on a gold mine?"

"Do you still have a lot of your dad's sixties furniture? Sure, if they're in good shape."

Amadeo grinned. "Could change the name of my ranch from the Lone Palm to the Chi Chi. Oh, here she is."

Willow looked adorable as she stumbled down the bluff. Her face was lit with a space-age glow from her cell phone as she read a text. "What the fuck?" she wondered in a hushed voice.

Then two men flanked her. "What is it?" asked Steffen.

Amadeo could see the fear in her eyes. "Jaclyn just stopped by the Searchlight to see me. She said we've been burglarized."

* * * *

Well, no one said life in California would be dull.

By the time Willow arrived back at her motel, the cops had taken the full report from Jaclyn and the worker Carl.

"And where was this foreman Chas White," asked the cop, "at the estimated time of the break-in?"

"Who the hell knows?" Carl glared at the cop. "Chas White is as rare as a stylish mullet! I'm basically the one in charge, if you want to pin responsibility on me. And I'm telling you, that door hasn't been opened in *years*. We've been accessing that room through the utility room, which was locked."

The burglar had entered the Cesar Romero Room by crowbarring the stuck front door, which now sat askew, splintered, the hinges crimped. Willow entered to try and discern which items had been stolen. Immediately she noticed the nightstand didn't hold the silk-inlaid Ben Wa box anymore. Luckily, the balls were still inside her, rolling against each other as though she were having one long continuous orgasm.

But she couldn't tell the cops about that, or the missing mop flogger. Looking some more, she noticed the cat o'nine tails was also gone, along with some leather straps or harnesses they hadn't gotten around to yet. They were going to move everything into the Gadabout Gaddis Cottage. So Willow had to lamely tell the cop, "I really don't notice anything missing."

Steffen sliced the air with his hand and told the cop, "It's that Ronnie Dobbs moron, Tony. Amadeo here and I just put a BOLO out on him two days ago and it obviously didn't work. You can dust for prints all you want, but he's such an experienced criminal I'm sure he wore gloves."

"Yeah, I'm not finding much," called the technician who was dusting.

Carl chuckled. "Aside from Cesar Romero's prints. I wonder how long prints last?" The cop looked at him oddly, so Carl sobered up and told him, "Look. I agree, it's this Ronnie Dobbs dickhead. Just last month he was inflating a monster truck tire over in Beaumont but got distracted by some titty magazine. Tire exploded from being over-inflated, piece of scrap metal nearly sliced the arm off another dude working nearby. I tell you, this project has Ronnie Dobbs written all over it."

Tony sighed. "But as far as you can discern, nothing was taken. And this is the only room broken into."

Willow felt horrible having to tell the cop, "Yes, the only room. No, nothing." The old Ben Wa box, whip, and mop flogger were probably only valued at about twenty dollars, and no cop would even waste time looking for that culprit. She was surprised, overall, that they were even dusting for prints.

Steffen told Tony, "But I want to put out a restraining order on this asshat."

Tony said, "You do know that sometimes that backfires. Sometimes it enrages the suspect even more. I'm familiar enough with Dobbs to think he might fall into this category. He's kind of a loose cannon. He was getting drunk with his brother once a couple years ago out in the desert, and the brother shot him. Ronnie fell onto a rattlesnake and was bitten."

Willow—and other people including Carl—couldn't help but laugh. It probably wasn't proper, laughing at a guy being bitten by a rattlesnake, but hell, he had just stolen her Ben Wa box. She told

Officer Tony, "You know, there *was* one thing missing, so tiny I didn't mention it. It was in this nightstand, and it was an old antique, silk-covered box. That's it. I know Dobbs was here looking for old mid-century artifacts—he thought I had some wristwatch and he wanted to buy it, so he could have thought the box was valuable."

"A box," repeated Tony, bored already.

Steffen pointed at Tony. "Yes. Red, with two circular indentations inside, to carry…circular objects."

"Objects," repeated Tony dully, writing. "Circular. So if you want to follow through on the restraining order, come down to the station tomorrow."

Carl said, "Ronnie doesn't seem to mind being arrested. It doesn't deter him. It's like a freak flag he likes to fly."

"Right," said Officer Tony. "He likes to brag about being 'the most arrested man in the Coachella Valley.' Which he *is*, at last count."

After the cops left, Carl insisted on sticking around as a security guard—for an additional fee, of course. Willow didn't think that was necessary, but Steffen and Amadeo seemed to think it was excellent.

"Without Carl, you're the only person sleeping in this entire building," Amadeo pointed out. "And I don't like that."

"Right," agreed Steffen. "Willow, he took your whip and flogger and God knows what else. Did you even know what was in this room? There were some old clothes in that chest of drawers that seem to be missing."

"Right," said Carl with authority. "And there was a banging leather head harness hanging in that closet that isn't there anymore."

Everyone stared at Carl. Carl held his hands up innocently and slunk back a few feet.

"What we're trying to say is," said Amadeo, "I think we should take Carl up on his offer. Or you spend the night at my ranch."

"I'm fine here," insisted Willow. "I get up at five in the morning to start work, or I'd take up your ranch offer, Amadeo. Carl, can we start tomorrow relocating this equipment and furniture into the Gadabout Gaddis Cottage?"

Carl hooked a thumb at the wall. "Gadabout Gaddis? You mean that gentleman on TV who flew around to different lakes fishing was a client of this place in the day? Good for him! I guess he wasn't called a 'gadabout' for no reason. Yeah, sure, Miss Paige, no problem. The painting in the cottage has been done and the carpet installed, so no problem moving the furniture in. I can upgrade the security on the cottage, too, to include alarms if anyone breaks any of the windows. Only a couple more bucks a month per window."

"Cool," agreed Willow. "You'll sleep here, then?"

"Absolutely," said Carl. "You never know when thieves return to the scene of a crime. He might be coming back for one of those furry blindfolds in that drawer. For all you know, it could be as rare as a Billy Ray Cyrus hit song."

The men stared at the worker with narrowed eyes, but Willow snickered and stepped over the wood splinters and into the hallway. Her own suite, the Ocean's 11 Room, was up a flight of steps past the office. The men insisted on walking her upstairs to her door.

"I'd like to know Dobbs' end game," said Amadeo. "It can't possibly just be that wristwatch. There's *got* to be something in here that's valuable."

"Yeah," said Steffen. "Carl's halfway right. You never know when some furry blindfold turns out to be worth a hundred grand. I've got a collection, myself, of fairly trivial stuff that's been valued for amazing sums."

Willow had never been to Steffen's house, but she could imagine that in his travels around the Coachella Valley he collected some worthwhile things. "What do you collect?"

Steffen seemed to regret having said anything. "Oh, entertainment memorabilia. My point is—"

"Liberace," it sounded as though Amadeo said from behind his hand, but he coughed at the same time.

"Liberace?" Willow tried to clarify. "You mean that flamboyant pianist who—"

"Yeah, yeah." Steffen tried to wave away the word "Liberace." "That stuff is valuable, no matter *whose* memorabilia it is. And Ronnie Dobbs is such a whack-a-mole it's entirely possible he's still looking for Norman Fell's stupid wristwatch and is just stealing everything else that isn't nailed down."

"I think there's more to it than that," said Willow thoughtfully. "Ronnie Dobbs is a fairly random guy, but I think there might actually be a method to his madness. Come by tomorrow. Check out the Gadabout Cottage once Carl moves everything in."

She kissed Amadeo goodbye. She felt like a tiny sparrow in his arms, which was better than feeling like a "thunder thighs." When she kissed Steffen, she chided him. "Liberace."

He held her at arm's length. "Hey. You should count your blessings. At least I'm not looking for Norman Fell's wristwatch."

The men waited until she was in her suite and had locked her door. She threw her bag on the coffee table, and her cell phone slid out. She noticed she had a voice mail. She held it scrunched between her ear and shoulder as she yanked open her fridge door to find that open bottle of white wine she thought was already in there.

She had yanked out the cork but froze when she heard Matt's tinny, recorded voice. "Willow. Ah, I just want to say, ah, I…I really feel like an asshole about the other day, how I acted when you tried to tell me about Stormy. I'm really sorry that I was so distracted about some business that I didn't give you my full attention. I came across like I was insensitive. For that I apologize." Matt inhaled and exhaled, as though an enormous weight had been lifted now that he'd officially apologized. But for some reason it didn't really *feel* like a sincere, true apology, and Willow waited for more flowery words or sentiments.

Nothing like that came.

Matt continued. "I was just all occupied with some urgent business." He tried to laugh. "You know how it is, no doubt, with your new business venture and all. Anyway, I'll really miss Stormy. She was the best. Take care."

Willow stared at the phone as if it was somehow responsible for leaving out the truly sincere part of the voice mail. But no, that was the whole thing, apparently. Matt didn't say "I apologize for *being* an asshole and honestly not giving a flying fuck about you or Stormy," no, he just felt bad that he had *looked* like an asshole, probably in front of whatever bimbo he was banging. Maybe the bimbo had asked "who was that and what did she want," and when Matt was forced to tell her about the dog, the bimbo had chided him for actually *being* insensitive. Not "seeming" insensitive.

Willow poured her wine and drank it, drifting to the slider that led to the patio. A couple of faraway remote lights twinkled in the valley underneath the dark purple silhouette of the San Jacinto Mountains. They were probably all buildings of Amadeo's Lone Palm Ranch.

A week ago, that asshole message from Matt would have upset Willow beyond all measure. But right now, maybe because she had had a long exhausting day, she really didn't give a shit.

That's Matt's loss if he's so callous he can't really love a dog. Or me.

Maybe only when you stopped caring about one thing were you able to start caring about something new.

Chapter Ten

"I'm not going to ask why you want me to bolt these shackles to this pool table."

"You're a smart one, Carl," said Willow.

The St. Andrew's Cross had been installed in the Gadabout Cottage. There had been a pool table in excellent condition in her Ocean's 11 Room when Willow had first moved in, so she had just had it removed down to the cottage. The pool table fit in perfectly with the swinging motif. Steffen was already calling the cottage "our mid-century oasis."

Steffen was becoming an invaluable asset. With his architectural and design knowledge, Willow had incorporated about a hundred of his suggestions, not just into the cottage, but all over the Searchlight Motel. Just today he had even sheepishly brought over a framed poster of a sequined Liberace for the Gadabout Cottage. He had explained that it was the only memorabilia he owned that a guest might not steal. The poster frame's pumpkin orange even matched the plastic seat covers of the modular dining room set.

Carl's electric screwdriver whirred as he attached the shackles to the head rail of the pool table. "I can't figure out if these are for wrists or ankles. I got to give you that. I just don't understand, I guess. How are the cops going to believe you if you ever get robbed again if you're already tied up?"

"You just leave that up to us, Carl," Steffen said soothingly. He was finishing up installing a new gas range in the kitchenette.

Carl wouldn't, though. He did love to talk. "I mean, is this up to code? What kind of liability insurance are you going to carry, Miss Paige?"

Willow was supposed to be working at the table on her laptop surfing for venetian blinds, but she was really looking at Steffen. He lay on his back fiddling with something on the stove. With his arms over his head, his shirt hiked up, revealing an enticing strip of taut, bare abdomen. "You know, Carl," she said distantly, "if you ever feel like switching jobs, come work for me. Jaclyn keeps harassing me to hire her Fernando as the motel handyman, but I don't trust that guy's work ethic. He's always too busy lounging at her house watching the Gladiator Channel, some old sword-and-sandals epic."

"More like a *socks* and sandals epic," said Steffen. "That guy has absolutely no sense of style. Always wearing socks with his Birkenstocks."

A laugh escaped Willow's lips. Steffen was right. Not only did Fernando cultivate the Bozo hairstyle as if it was some new trend, he *did* have unfortunate choice in footgear in addition to his Bermuda shorts. "He must have some good traits, Steffen," she called out, trying to be fair. "He does seem fairly mellow and easygoing."

"I just talked to Tony Pickett," said Amadeo as he breezed into the cottage. Willow looked over, surprised he was there. She knew he was supposed to be overseeing the baling of hay, or some such cattle ranching thing. "He verified that Ronnie Dobbs had just been released from jail two hours before the break-in."

Willow wanted to forget about Ronnie Dobbs. She was sure he would just move on to whatever caught his eye next, like falling into a wood chipper or smoking some poison oak. She felt much more secure with Carl around, too. She had already advertised her motel's grand opening in several places and had included a date, so she wanted to ignore Mr. Dobbs. She had no time for him. "That's no indication of anything, really. Did they get print results back?"

Amadeo nodded sternly. "Yeah. The *only* prints in the room belonged to the three of us." He cast his narrowing eyes at Carl, who peeked innocently over the head rail. "And the fingerprints of some guy named Carl Bogart. *His* prints were in the database due to some St. Patrick's Day drunk and disorderly."

Carl half-rose from behind the table. "It was a *police* horse I was kissing! Why'd they arrest me for kissing their own *horse?*"

Amadeo's gaze was steely, but Willow and Steffen laughed. Steffen sat up straight on the kitchenette floor. He looked manlier than ever holding a wrench. "Question is, Carl. Why were your prints in the room at all?"

Carl's eyes grew wider. "I had to clean the mirrors, didn't I? Cesar Romero wouldn't tolerate dust-covered mirrors."

Willow got up from the table. The venetian blinds could wait—Steffen was looking just too, too delicious. He sat blinking in the middle of a block of sun that flooded one of the cottage's many windows. A "long cool drink of water," that's how she had thought of him the first time she'd seen him. Already she knew him so intimately. She knew he hated celery yet was mostly a vegetarian, owned a tropical salt water fish tank, had an American father who was a Lieutenant Colonel in the army, and came almost instantly when his balls were licked.

Now, knowing he'd been the high school quarterback, Willow marveled at how things changed. In Florida she had been neither with the "in" or the "out" crowd. She had just been a slightly overweight but pretty girl who hung around on the fringes. She started smoking cigarettes to look cool, lost the weight, and got a degree from the community college. Everything was fairly middle-of-the-road for her until she met the handsome Matt at that door company. She had been amazed he had seemed to want her, and she even changed her perfume and toenail color to suit his likes.

That didn't seem necessary with the open, confident, relaxed Steffen Jung. He called her "shapely" and "supersonic," not "fat." Her only fear was that he'd tire of her. She knew he was accustomed to dating several women at once, and he'd told her in plain English that he liked "racy women." How long before he got bored with her? He might stick around until they got to the "Dessert Tray" on the Palomino Ranch's menu—when they were done trying out every piece of bondage furniture in the Gadabout Cottage.

And he claimed to have never had a relationship with another man, yet he seemed to plunge right into lovemaking with the virile Amadeo. Steffen held nothing back when he thrust his tongue down Amadeo's throat or gulped the strapping man's penis. She was suspicious of his talent when it came to women, sure, but that background was more obvious. Steffen loved women. He had a lot of experience. He was, after all, forty. After about age thirty, no one was kidding anyone if they pretended they were *not* experienced. But Steffen seemed to lust for the former high school loser Amadeo with almost equal enthusiasm as he lusted for her. He must have a steamier background than he let on. Or, it might be possible he simply liked Amadeo as much as he liked her.

She reached a hand out for Steffen to take. Thank God he had signed off his approval on the newly installed air conditioning, because it was over a hundred degrees outside. "Come on. Is the stove installed all right? Let's try out that pool table." He clasped his hand around her wrist and let her help him up.

"That's my sign to exit." Carl was unplugging his screwdriver. "I don't need to see no eight-ball in the corner pocket."

Willow and Steffen looked quizzically at each other. Had Carl been reading the menu too? It was likely just an accidental pun, though, and Willow told Carl, "After your lunch, can you check on the sign installers?" Her retro neon "Searchlight Motel" sign was being installed out front. Lots of people had already stopped to take photographs, some of them probably newspapermen.

Carl left, and Amadeo said, "You should get out front and pose before your new sign. Good publicity."

Steffen sat Willow down on the rail of the pool table. “I really don’t think she needs publicity, Amadeo. This place is right on Manilow Avenue. I know this part of Last Chance has been pretty dead since the sixties when they rerouted the highway, but it’s been up and coming the past few years. They’ve got that new organic store, green store, card store—”

“The Racquet Club,” Amadeo added with a crooked smile.

Steffen was already taking a deep bite from the side of Willow’s neck. When he squiggled his tongue near her jugular vein, the shiver that raced down her spine plumped her pussy lips. Steffen was handy with the ladies, that was for sure. Suspiciously handy. “You’re sublime,” he murmured. Then, louder, he said “And the newspaper offices, new fire station, that office building—”

Behind Steffen, Amadeo was already stripping off his wifebeater shirt. Willow didn’t blame him for going shirtless at every possible opportunity. A group from Steffen’s Modern Committee had stopped by to see the remodeling progress, and several women had assumed Amadeo was a cabana boy. He didn’t dissuade them from thinking that, either. He’d hung out at her outdoor Atomic Café, which actually *was* a poolside cabana, mixing drinks with rum and coconut milk for the women. “And the Racquet Club. I’m telling you, that club is the number one draw in the downtown area.”

“You can go to the Racquet Club.” Steffen’s breath warmed Willow’s neck and stiffened her nipples against the bra of her skimpy slip dress. “I have no need to go there anymore.”

His words warmed Willow’s heart. Dared she hope? She knew that she wanted to be monogamous with the men—or was that “polyamorous”?—but it was too much to expect them to feel the same. Men were dogs. At the slightest sign of a complication, they withdrew emotionally, if not physically. She kissed Steffen’s seductive mouth and twined her sandals around the backs of his knees. “We have our own Racquet Club here.”

"Yeah, yeah," Amadeo continued dismissively. "I'm just saying that the traffic going to and from the Racquet Club, the word of mouth, is enough to get you business. Especially for your new Gadabout Cottage."

Steffen said, "I'll gadabout *you*, buddy, if you don't get up on this table and get your dick in her mouth. We're spit roasting *her* today."

"*Ooh*," Willow cooed, although she didn't really know what Steffen referred to.

She knew that their experience near the Kupka House the other day was called a Spit Roast. The person in the middle, in that case Steffen, was skewered from two ends by two different people. Willow now had a new erotic fantasy, if she ever needed to fire up her trusty vibrator again. The image of the two young men in Daytona Beach was forever erased from her memory banks now that a new image had taken its place. Steffen bent over, subservient on his knees as he lapped away at her pussy, penetrated from the rear by that sensuously brutal cowboy. The memory was seared onto the backs of her eyelids. How Steffen's moans had vibrated deep inside her uterus when Amadeo lunged his penis inside him. How she could reach out and touch her fingertips to Amadeo's smooth chest, his pectorals flexing as he gripped his lover by the hips. How she could even tell when Steffen was coming, spilling his seed over Amadeo's fingers as her clitoris quivered against his tongue.

Never. Never had she experienced anything like it.

The memories spurred her on now. "I thought you didn't want me, ah, interacting with Amadeo," she whispered against his ear. Meanwhile, Amadeo was eagerly stripping, flinging his clothes right and left with abandon, even though the windows had no covering and workers were passing by the cottage.

Amadeo must have had the ears of a rabbit. He coiled his naked torso around Steffen's and eagerly began unbuttoning his shirt from behind. "Yeah. What's up with this sudden change of mind?" he growled, impatiently fingering Steffen's nipples.

Steffen shook his shoulders like a dog shaking off rain. "Why are you questioning it? Get up there and enjoy it."

Amadeo was clearly torn between taking his palms off Steffen's chiseled pecs or jumping onto the table to do Steffen's bidding. Naked now, he humped Steffen's hip with a cock so hard it was up against his navel. He had torn off Steffen's shirt, so Willow could feel Steffen's velvety skin, the wiriness of his chest hair against her bosom as he leaned over her.

Steffen slid both hands around her ass that was perched on the edge of the table rail. He opened her up like splitting a peach, rimming her bulging pussy lips with his fingertips. She knew she was already juicy as a peach, too, the way his fingers slithered up and down her clitoris, expertly lingering on the spot he knew was the most effective.

She purred, "Will we try the Two Ball?"

They had noted a menu item called "Two Ball in the Corner Pocket" but had no idea what it was. Since there had been a pool table on the bordello property, they conjectured that it had something to do with that, and had just invented a new description for it. Willow knew it would involve penetration, and she had never felt Steffen's cock inside her. Now, she was eager. She found if she raised one knee toward the ceiling and balanced herself on the rail by wedging her heel there, she could reach around and tickle the root of Steffen's cock with her fingertips. In his eagerness, Amadeo had unsheathed his lover's cock, but was generously directing it toward Willow.

Amadeo answered for Steffen. "Two ball her," he urged. "Right into the corner pocket."

At the moment Steffen slid his prick into her wet pussy, Willow gasped. She had just remembered. If she was the roastee and Steffen was penetrating her vaginally, she would have to take Amadeo's member into her mouth.

Dear God. As if Steffen alone isn't enough.

But her boyfriend encouraged her. “There,” he said soothingly, seating himself deep inside her as though he had all the time in the world. She heard him slap Amadeo’s ass as the cowboy clambered onto the rail, straddling her. When she opened her eyes, she was face-to-face with a long, hard dick that emanated the scent of leather. “There. You can handle us both at the same time.”

* * * *

Of course, Steffen had been dying to slide his prick up the sultry motel owner’s pussy. He just hadn’t expected to be doing it so soon, without much warning. It just all came together at once when she’d pulled him up from the kitchen floor, suggesting they reenact Two Ball in the Corner Pocket. Before he’d had a chance to whip out a condom he’d been carrying in his wallet, boom. His dick had a mind of its own, and he had penetrated Willow.

He’d been suspecting he was in love with her since the moment he’s first seen her in her office. Steffen hadn’t *wanted* to fall in love again. He’d been in love with the two women he’d imagine he would marry, and look how *that* had turned out. No. It was much better to just casually hook up with women, leaving if he started to feel anything for them.

This time, though, he was going to see it through. Maybe it was the interesting addition of Amadeo the horny cowboy that was encouraging Steffen to stick around. It had turned Steffen on beyond belief to realize he was being idolized by someone who had longed to suck his tool since perving on him taking a shower decades ago. Who didn’t like being idolized? And his passionate feelings for Amadeo went beyond the physical. He had a genuine respect for the brutal, straightforward rancher. It didn’t hurt that he knew Amadeo looked at him with desire, but even just sharing a meal with the guy was enjoyable. Steffen was bringing Amadeo around to his way of thinking about architecture, too. He wanted to look at Amadeo’s ranch house with fresh eyes. It had been built in the fifties with walls of glass, incorporating a few existing boulders as well.

Now Steffen took a rest, seated inside her, waiting for Amadeo to position himself. Almost idly, he tried out the ankle shackle Carl had bolted to the table. *Perfect.* Willow purred with pleasure when he buckled the leather strap around her ankle. His cock twitched deep inside her as Amadeo straddled her, kneeling on the table's bed. She leaned back on the cloth on her palms, and Steffen had the perfect view of Amadeo's shapely ass as he waggled his delicious cock in Willow's face.

Steffen was torn about allowing his woman to suck Amadeo's cock. But he would have to face it eventually if he wanted to keep playing with both of them. He could, of course, be that sort of Dom who didn't allow play between the other two. Willow would tire of that, no doubt, and Amadeo would become frustrated as well. No, he had to allow Amadeo to insert that velvety cock between Willow's plush lips. There was really no "allowing" going on at all. It was just going to happen.

As Amadeo gyrated his prick into Willow's mouth, Steffen slapped the ass that was presented to him. He barely had to move at all inside Willow in order to feel on the verge of coming, so he distracted himself. Gripping the muscular mounds of Amadeo's ass, Steffen parted them and buried his face. If he reached his tongue out as far as possible, he could lap away at Amadeo's perineum. Yes, he could even suck on it, the balls swaying near his chin, his mouth close to Willow's.

He had an idea. Licking a finger, he inserted the first knuckle up Amadeo's asshole. Steffen found that he could tickle the slick anus while sucking on the perineum. If Amadeo was anything like him, he'd soon be driven over the edge of bliss. That would shorten the amount of time Amadeo was fucking his girlfriend's mouth.

Amadeo, as the only person with his mouth not full, was able to groan and shiver with delight. "That's perfect," he moaned. "Willow, keep sucking my dick. We're gonna spit roast you till you're tender and juicy, hear? Steffen's gonna give you a nice cream pie. His dick's nice and fat and hefty, isn't it? Use your tongue, mistress. Put your tongue into it. *Ah!*"

Steffen swelled with pride when he obviously found Amadeo's prostate. He'd never finger-banged another man before. But he knew where *he* liked to be massaged, and he found that spot inside Amadeo. Stroking the slick gland, Steffen murmured to Willow, "You're doing good. Feel my cock about to explode inside of you? You're doing good, sweetie. You feel so nice and tight around my cock, you voluptuous minx. You're taking two men at once and doing a good job." Remembering her Daytona Beach fantasy, he added, "My finger stroking Amadeo's ass is going to help him come quicker in your mouth. Get ready. Get ready for a big cowboy load—*ah!*"

It was Steffen who was taken by surprise. The blissful shivers that had been coaxing his penis on toward orgasm finally came to a head. As Amadeo's anus clamped down around his massaging finger, Steffen found his cock rupturing in ecstasy deep inside Willow's heat. With her shackled ankles up on the rails like that he could wedge his cockhead up against her cervix. He saw she was able to swallow all of Amadeo's load, unlike the time he had flooded her little mouth. Amadeo's ass muscles flexed as he drained himself inside the sweet girl's mouth.

Steffen's entire body quivered like a mass of jelly. His legs even began giving out, although Willow held herself up on the pool table. As much as he hated to, he had to withdraw. He staggered to the kitchenette to wash his hands, casting glances at the burly cowboy who was still fucking his girlfriend's mouth.

"Hey." Steffen slapped the athletic ass. Then again, harder. "Out. Give the poor girl a rest." He unbuckled the shackles as Amadeo finally pulled his dripping dick from her mouth. Steffen slowly helped one of her feet to touch the ground, then the other, as she panted from her exertion. He knew about aftercare from living with that Domme—and hanging around the Racquet Club. They had to let Willow down slowly.

"Ah." She smiled weakly. "I'm fine."

"Are you all right? Here, pull down your pretty dress and sit on this couch."

"I have to go pee."

"All right. Go pee." He helped her as though she was infirm, and she shut the bathroom door. Buckling his jeans around his hips, he went to stand by Amadeo. He was at a plate glass window allowing the sun to bathe his naked torso, chuckling at a couple of workers who were looking at them oddly.

Amadeo said, "Did Willow order those blinds yet? We might want to just get some from Home Depot just to install them faster. Way to go on the Cream Pie, bro. Eiffel Tower!" He high-fived Steffen. It wasn't a true Eiffel Tower, though, when the woman was in the bathroom.

"Yeah, well." Steffen cleared his throat. "I feel kind of guilty about that. Going bareback and all. It's pretty insensitive of me not to roll on a rubber. I had one. I just suddenly got carried away."

Amadeo shrugged. "You love her," he stated, matter-of-factly.

How did Amadeo know that? Steffen regarded his lover. "I think I do, yeah. Do you love her?"

Amadeo's eyes sparkled. "I think I do, yeah."

Steffen snorted skeptically. "We'll see about that."

"Right. You're such a competitive bastard. We'll soon see which one of us she loves the most."

"You're on," agreed Steffen, as Willow emerged from the bathroom.

Chapter Eleven

Willow worried.

After her medical dilemmas when married to Matt, she was almost entirely certain she couldn't get pregnant again. Still, it was foolish to tempt fate like that. *Fucking without a rubber! What was I thinking?*

Still, since when were men expected to take control over that aspect of sex? Since never. Women who relied on men to handle birth control wound up in dire straits. She had been lax figuring out some sort of protection—probably because she was 99 percent certain she couldn't get pregnant again.

When she came out of the bathroom, Steffen immediately picked up on her change of mood. Maybe it was because she instantly headed for the wet bar and started making gin gimlets. He came up behind her, putting a hand on her shoulder. "Are you all right?"

She forced a smile. "Why wouldn't I be? That was an amazing session. And we tested out the ankle shackles. They work fine."

Steffen elbowed her aside. "Let me. I need to provide you with aftercare, not the other way around. I feel like an ass. I had a rubber in my wallet and suddenly things just got away from me. I need to apologize."

So he *had* thought about protection. Willow's heart melted. She stroked his arm. "Oh, it's no big deal," she said truthfully. "I doubt I can get pregnant, anyway. Oh, I don't need lime juice in mine."

"Then it's just a martini." Steffen handed her the cocktail glass anyway. "Here. Eat these chocolates, too. You need the sugar. What's this about not being able to get pregnant?"

She sipped and hugged herself. She looked sideways out a window. Workers kept peering inside. She needed to get a move on installing those blinds. "Oh, when I was married before, I had a miscarriage. There were some complications. No big deal, really, but a doctor told me more than likely I probably couldn't conceive again."

Suddenly Amadeo was standing there too. "'No big deal'? A miscarriage is a big deal." Willow had forgotten—Amadeo was a rancher. He knew about this sort of thing. "How far along were you?"

Willow shrugged. "Twenty weeks."

Amadeo's mouth was agape. "Twenty weeks? Hell, that's almost a viable baby." He wiped his face with his hand. "Oh, jeez. I'm sorry. I'm sure you don't need me to rustle up any bad memories."

Willow patted Amadeo's arm, too. "It's all right. You didn't know. That actually wasn't even the bad part. I think the really bad part was that the baby had already been dead inside of me, but I had to wait and go into the hospital to deliver it."

"They had to induce labor," Amadeo intoned.

"Right." Willow hadn't talked about this incident in ages. Not since she'd described it and its aftermath to Jaclyn about four months ago. "It was a 'delayed miscarriage.' The entire placenta wasn't expelled, so I had complications—oh, God, I don't want to squidge you out."

"No one's squidged out," Steffen insisted. "I had a girlfriend have a miscarriage once. I think it's why we broke up, when I'd thought we were going to get married. She could never feel the same about me again and sort of withdrew. I didn't understand it."

"Exactly!" Willow pointed at Steffen with her cocktail glass. "I withdrew afterward, not just from Matt but from everything. I never went back to my job, for example."

"It's devastating," Steffen agreed. "Men tend to move on in life and not dwell on things—to sort of ignore things—and women want to mull it over and digest it. We don't understand each other."

"Right. Well, not only did Matt not understand it, he became so *angry* at me for withdrawing. He just raged about everything, and then *he* withdrew from *me.*" It wasn't Willow's intention to sob about her first husband to her current lovers. There was nothing more unattractive than someone with unresolved issues from a prior relationship. So she gulped her drink, and the glass was soon empty.

Steffen said, "That sounds like what happened with me and my ex. I didn't understand her, so it was painful to be around her. I thought maybe she blamed me for the miscarriage in some way. Like maybe I had bad genes, or maybe we shouldn't have fucked so hard." He stroked Willow's cheek, and she realized her face was wet.

What? Am I crying? What the fuck? How embarrassing. She tried to laugh it off. "Well, don't compare yourself to my ex, Steffen. You're nothing alike. He responded by never coming home, fucking other bimbos, and losing himself in drugs and partying."

"Well." Steffen shrugged. "I can't say my reaction was completely different. Maybe minus the drugs."

"Oh, there's not even a vague comparison. Believe you me, Steffen." Willow went to the table and rooted around in her giant bag. She didn't know what she was looking for—a nonexistent cigarette, maybe—but she knew she didn't like Steffen comparing himself to Matt. She understood that he was trying to stand up for the male side of the equation, to admit culpability in the age-old war between the sexes, but Matt had just been a horribly immature asshole who had been doing bimbos and drugs before she'd even gotten pregnant.

Over at the bar, Amadeo said, "Maybe she doesn't want to talk about it, bro. Not the kind of bonding women want after a good fucking."

Willow waved a dismissive hand. "It's all right, Amadeo. I'm not much for any sappy bonding, anyway."

Amadeo came toward the table. "It's not so much the sappy bonding, but you probably don't know that after a kink session it's a good idea to come down slowly. Aftercare, it's called."

Willow scoffed. She *wanted* to be as callous and unfeeling as men always seemed to be. "That wasn't much of a kink session. Hardly anyone got spanked, and only my ankles were shackled to the table."

Amadeo smiled crookedly. "Believe me, Willow. You might think you're fine, but you might find yourself sobbing in an hour or two if you don't let us care for you."

"Ha," said Willow. "If there's any sobbing it's because you two clods were congratulating each other with an Eiffel Tower while I was in the bathroom." She said it lightly, and was really only slightly annoyed having overheard them high-fiving over their sex act, but she slung her bag over her shoulder and picked up her laptop.

"Whoa, now!" said Steffen, coming toward her with palms out like a crossing guard. "Willow, don't leave. Amadeo is right—you need aftercare whether you know it or not. I've seen women leave the club seeming fine, then get discovered crying in their cars hours later in the parking lot."

Now Willow truly *was* miffed. "Enough with your damned women in clubs, Steffen!" she cried harshly. "Did it ever occur to you that maybe I don't *want* to hear about your sleazy past? Just because you're a man you think it's incredibly fun and funny, but guess what? Most women don't agree."

As she sailed out the door—wondering if she should slam it for a grand exit—she heard Amadeo saying, "See, bro? She's already sub-dropping. I'm going after her."

Willow twirled around on the walkway and called breezily, "I'm fine, Amadeo. I'm just going to go out front to check on the sign installation. I'll get Carl or whoever to go pick up the venetian blinds at Home Depot."

The last thing she heard was Steffen standing at the door telling Amadeo, "Maybe this is her way after sex. Maybe she withdraws and wants to hide."

He's right about that.

* * * *

Willow decided to accompany Carl to pick up the blinds. Afterwards she actually had to stop by City Hall to attend to some permit bullshit. Seeing Steffen's coworkers milling about so studiously sent a fresh surge of love rushing through Willow's chest.

Yes, love. She'd been suspecting for awhile now that she was falling in love with the Chief Building Inspector, but she had tried to block it from her thoughts. She didn't want to repeat the sappy, mindless sort of slavish "love" she had experienced with Matt—the sort of obsession that ruined one's sleep and made one change their toenail polish color. She had suffered for *years* wondering and anguishing over every word of Matt's, every nonsensical, assholish, immature word. If that was love, she didn't need it. She needed to sleep once in awhile.

Willow was also leery of Steffen's womanizing history. Shouldn't she suspect any man who reached the age of forty without being at least divorced? He must have some fear of intimacy. Sure, he was gorgeous and chiseled—he could get away with it. And what man wouldn't get away with whatever he could, for as long as possible? A man would be a moron not to take advantage of it.

Yet Willow could muster no respect for that sort of superficial womanizing user. Did she only imagine she loved Steffen for his chiseled Teutonic looks? That made her equally superficial.

She knew it went beneath the surface, her passionate feelings for him. It wasn't just his seductive grin, his erotic, tapered fingers, his natural oaky scent. Willow sincerely loved Steffen's gadabout Army history, his football playing, his yoga. She even loved his abstinence from red meat, although eating it was one of her true thrills left in life. She shared his interest in giant, fluffy dogs, botany, dinosaur skeletons, country music, and the televised guilty pleasures of men flailing about in swamps. Willow adored his laugh, his messy work truck, and his modern architecture. In fact, there wasn't one aspect of Steffen Jung that annoyed her.

Aside from his handy way with the ladies. How could she ever compete with the hordes of slender Palm Springs party women, all waiting in line to hand Steffen their phone number? She would feel insecure forever next to them.

She wasn't really upset that her two lovers had Eiffel Towered each other while she was in the bathroom. That was men for you. Willow was upset because she was in love with Steffen but she felt he would never truly be hers. The resurgence of her pain at the miscarriage had brought a sudden swell of sadness and loss over the whole mess, and suddenly she had to get away from the men. What was Amadeo talking about, "sub-drop"? Why had Steffen handed her chocolate? What was "aftercare"? They had hardly been whipping each other or swinging from the chandelier or whatever bondage people normally did at that beloved club of Steffen and Amadeo's. No one had been strapped to the St. Andrew's Cross or spanked on the spanking bench.

Yet as she went about her day, she felt as though she was horribly hung over. Could one gimlet have done that to her? She was awash with emotion, practically ripping one of Chas White's workers a new one because he spilled some paint on a walkway. She had dinner with Jaclyn at Sprockets and was relieved to return to the Searchlight around ten and see Steffen's and Amadeo's trucks both missing from the parking lot. There were only a few worker's trucks remaining, one of them Carl's. He was probably at the Gadabout Cottage installing the blinds and had asked some coworkers to help.

"Steffen and Amadeo are probably out at the Racquet Club," she muttered as she unlocked the glass door to her office. Mail had been shoved through the slot, spreading out in a fan on the floor. It was amazing how much mail a business could get before its grand opening.

Not wanting to mess up her desk further, Willow stood by the recycling box, tossing catalogues and tire coupons into it. She felt sad and empty—almost emptier than she had at any point since arriving in Last Chance months ago. She realized why. It was *she* who had withdrawn from Steffen and Amadeo, though the worst thing they had done was congratulated each other on having spit roasted her on a pool table. That was hardly anything to get all up in arms about.

Why had she withdrawn after they'd been so intimate? Because Steffen wasn't the marrying sort? Willow realized that maybe she felt vulnerable, wide open. Not only had she literally bared herself and her thunder thighs on a pool table, she had told them what had caused the ruin of her marriage. *Damn! Can't I keep anything to myself? What made me think they would care about my stupid past troubles?* Willow was now mad at herself for having laid herself so wide open to the men. Men didn't care about stuff like that. Men wanted women to shut up and fuck.

It's all my fault. I need to be more cheerful around them. I wouldn't blame them if they decided to shitcan me. What do they need me for? They could go to the Racquet Club together and play with both men and women.

Willow almost tossed the last envelope into the recycling box. She did a double take when she realized it was from the state of Florida. Gripping it, she tore it open and read:

Final Judgment of Dissolution of Marriage

Holy shit! Her divorce was final, at last.

Willow slowly sank into her rolling office chair, staring at the form. This was what she had wanted, but now it made her feel even emptier, if such a thing was possible. Eight years of her life down the tubes, a waste, all for nothing. Now she was thirty-two and most likely infertile. Who wanted an infertile wife? She had still loved Matt when she had forced herself to leave him and file for divorce. After two years of him shutting her out emotionally and physically, she had finally accepted defeat. Now even this small triumph—being the Petitioner in the divorce—felt empty.

Sighing heavily, Willow stood. She'd go up to her Ocean's 11 Room and watch one of the redneck reality shows she taped but never had a chance to watch. Open a bottle of wine. Try to convince herself that Steffen and Amadeo weren't dumping her.

She was gathering her giant laptop bag when someone came busting through the office door. He hit the door with such force it banged against the wall before slamming shut again. Willow gasped loudly and jumped a foot in the air, inadvertently tossing her bag aside.

"All right, you thieving slut!" The man crouched down low and aimed a bowie knife at her as though it was a pistol. "Hand it over!"

Willow assumed it was one of Carl's workers. Obviously, he had pounded a few too many and was mistaking her for someone else. "I think you have me confused with—"

"Shut up!" the guy yelled, advancing a step. "I just want that goddamned wrist cuff! You can keep all your fucking Ben Wa balls and feather dusters!"

Then it struck Willow. The guy who now resembled Ned Flanders, with an enormous mop of a fake moustache and a plastic Superman wig pasted to his head, was the guy who had formerly resembled Bart Simpson's bus driver. He even wore a green pullover sweater. *This is Ronnie Dobbs.* And he was resorting to some strange kind of violence to get whatever it was he wanted.

"Ronnie!" she said in a hushed voice, hoping to startle him into some kind of sobriety. "I never found any wristwatch! You need to stop breaking into *my* fucking hotel looking for something that just isn't here."

"I knew you'd say that." Ronnie sidled closer, holding the knifepoint at Willow's throat level, breathing Night Train all over her. He was a skinny, wormy thing, but it was Willow's experience that even the feeblest man was stronger than most women. That was the unfortunate truth. She remained frozen in position. "I've been up against lying, scheming bitches like you before. You don't scare me. Besides, it's no damned wristwatch I'm after. I just said that to see if you'd show me all your memorabilia."

It had all happened so fast, Willow didn't have time to be afraid. She felt as though she were viewing her body from outside, from somewhere up by the ceiling, remote and distant. "Well, it'd help if you'd tell me what you really wanted. And I would like that Ben Wa box back."

Apparently this was the wrong thing to say, for Ronnie now held the blade against her throat. "You ain't getting no damned box back! I mean, *what* box? Listen up! It's a leather wrist *cuff* I'm looking for, like something that would've been in your Cesar Romero room."

"Oh." Willow was a bit more timid now, and no longer felt so remote and bold. With the cold blade against her neck she felt as vulnerable as a lamb. "But you took everything in the Cesar Romero room."

Ronnie began to huff and puff, and Willow thought fast. Ronnie had stripped the Cesar Romero Room of anything that wasn't bolted down, but as far as she knew he hadn't broken into the Gadabout Cottage yet. "You know, I think I may have seen some leather cuffs in the cottage. You know where the cottage is, don't you?"

Ronnie laughed. "Sure I do. That's where you and those two beefcakes were getting as hot as a marathon runner's armpit. If I could transport that bondage cross I'd take that, too. You're such a stupid slut you didn't even know that thing is worth money."

"Okay, then. Let's go to the cottage."

"Okay. But I don't want to hear your gums a-flapping. If you think you can call out for one of your waxed ape-men you're dumber than I thought. Here, you damn slut." With one hand, Ronnie whipped off the necktie that hadn't been tied very well around his neck. Willow knew from watching those true stories about people who survived that it was usually the women who submitted or played dead who made it. It was hardly ever the women who fought back who prevailed, unfortunately. But intuitively her eyes scanned the room for anything she could use as a weapon. A hammer sat on a file cabinet on the other side of the room. But even if she managed to grab that, it would always be an uneven fight between a man and a woman. According to the shows, men only became more enraged if a woman tried to fight back.

However, apparently her body had the upper hand over her rational mind. When Ronnie plugged her mouth with the dirty, smelly tie, he had to use both hands to knot it behind her skull. He was forced to stick the knife into a pocket or other. "Course, this will only make you hotter than a red hen laying a goose egg, gagging you up like this. Heh. You're a spicy one. You sure can take those two muscle men. You sure got a pair of titties—"

When Ronnie jerked the knot tight and released it to reach for his knife, Willow made a break for the hammer. She lunged for it in one giant swoop, but Ronnie must have been accustomed to women who fought back. Just as her fingers closed around the handle of the hammer, Ronnie must have grabbed the necktie. Willow's head was snapped back with the sudden jerk, and the next thing she knew, she was dangling from Ronnie's feeble little arm like a severed head.

"I knew you'd try and pull something like that," he said, perfectly composed. "I was expecting it."

He allowed her to kneel. She panted, realizing she'd been holding her breath with the sudden terror of Ronnie's attack. Matt had terrified her in this way on several occasions. Sudden bursts of rage that seemed to come out of nowhere and had obviously been building up. Maybe three times he'd laid hands on her, all after the miscarriage, when communication between them had shut down.

She tried to talk, to explain to Ronnie that she would not try to protest anymore, but of course only muffled sounds came out. The metallic taste of blood soaked into her tongue.

"What? Oh, that's right, you've got a *gag* in your mouth!" Ronnie chortled, not in an evil villain sort of way, but as though he honestly was watching a sitcom where a giant mole stomped on a tiny village. Willow had thought him cartoonish and just a joke, but this sort of obliviousness was probably more terrifying.

Now he yanked on the tie, and she staggered to a stand. "Let's get on down to the cottage so you can show me where the leather wrist cuffs are." He shoved her toward the swinging glass door, and she opened it. Like in a corny movie, he said, "I don't want no funny business. I know gals like you. Always shoving your big fat weight around. I had a rough enough childhood without being brutalized by y'all fat cows. Nope, not me! Not ole Ronnie C. Dobbs, at your service! Why, I've got a booming business in celebrity memorabilia. I got Scott Baio's paper towel holder and Erik Estrada's socks, not to mention Bronson Pinchot's mailbox."

How would anyone know that was Scott Baio's paper towel holder? Willow wondered many things as she stumbled down the breezeway. She felt like a horse pulling little Ronnie Dobbs along by the necktie gagging her. *Even if it could be proven to be his, how much would Pinchot's mailbox be worth?* Dobbs's harangue made it clearer why he thought Norman Fell's leather cuff would be worth anything. *What, did Erik Estrada embroider his name onto his socks? What makes that pair different from any other pair?* On the bright side, she could probably give Dobbs any old leather cuff and pretend it was Norman Fells's.

Ronnie babbled on. "Just ask anyone in the greater Beaumont area. Ole Ronnie Dobbs has got the most primo memorabilia in So Cal! Why, one time I brokered the sale of a first pressing of that great David Soul album, *Playing to an Audience of One*. The bidding was fast and furious!"

"*Put down the weapon!*"

A cop had stepped out sideways from behind the cottage and was pointing a pistol right at Ronnie. Unfortunately, since Willow led him like a pony, she was actually a quite handy human shield. The cottage was lit up inside, half of the blinds hung, but quiet, as though someone had warned Carl and his men to leave.

Ronnie pressed the bowie knife blade against Willow's throat so firmly he pierced the skin, and a warm trickle of blood ran down between her breasts. "Never, Officer Pickett! I'm sick and tired of you trying to prevent an honest man such as myself from making an honest living!"

In lieu of answering, Officer Tony just shot at the ground about three feet from Ronnie. The shock of being shot at was probably behind Ronnie throwing Willow to the ground and dashing the opposite direction, into the darkness over by the pétanque court, Officer Tony in hot pursuit.

"Police brutality!" Ronnie yelled. "Y'all is brutalizing me!"

Willow sat up, holding her throat. Before she could slip the gag from her mouth Steffen was kneeling at her side, doing it for her.

"Jesus fucking Christ, Willow. Tony called me like I asked him to because some cop reported Dobbs' truck out front. You didn't recognize it? I tried calling you, but first there was no answer, and then Tony told me to stop trying, that he was just gonna move in and nab Dobbs."

Steffen went silent when a couple of shots were fired, coming from the parking lot.

"Police brutality!" Dobbs could still be heard railing. "Attica! Attica!"

Two more shots and a squeal of tires. Willow realized she must've been holding her breath, and Steffen as well, for they both exhaled when they heard a truck drive off.

"He got away?" Willow squeaked.

"Don't talk," said Steffen. "Do you have a first aid kit in your office?"

"Of course."

He helped her walk as though she was an arthritic old lady, and she had to shake his arm off. Tony's siren blared as he peeled off after

Dobbs. "We just got here," Steffen explained. "I can't believe Dobbs was stupid enough to drive his own truck and leave it in your parking lot."

Willow shook her head with wonder. "I can't believe he was stupid enough for a *lot* of things. I mean, *David Soul*?"

"Who? Listen, what else did he do to you? He didn't—"

"Touch me? No, he just kept raving about how he wants some leather wrist cuff. Turns out the wristwatch was just to throw us off, so we didn't realize we had some stupid valuable leather cuff. I won't rest tonight until I find that damned cuff."

"*No!*" Steffen practically yelled. "You're coming with me, missy. If that numb nuts got away again, I am *not* allowing you to sleep at the Searchlight. You hear me?"

"That's true," said Willow. "If he thought a David Soul album was valuable, the leather cuff probably isn't either. I was thinking of just finding any old leather cuff and telling him that was the one he wanted."

"Good thinking. But let's not take the chance, shall we?" Steffen opened the first aid box Willow had handed him, making her sit in her office chair. "You're coming with me back to my house."

As much as Willow liked the idea of finally seeing Steffen's house, she pointed out, "Is that really any safer? If Dobbs is dead set on collecting 'memorabilia,' didn't it occur to you he might be targeting you next?"

Steffen paused, a cotton ball in one hand. Turning around, he showed her that he had a pistol of some kind stuck into the waistband of his jeans. He continued cleaning her neck. "I wasn't about to run after that whack-a-mole unarmed. I'm not taking chances when it comes to my little filly."

So Willow had to agree. It would be plain stupid to attempt to stay at the Searchlight, not with Ronnie Dobbs still meandering about, playing air guitar or drowning in a water bed. It wasn't worth the risk. And she was dying to see what Steffen's house looked like.

Chapter Twelve

Steffen got up, showered, brushed his teeth, then went back to bed.

He couldn't resist spooning against Willow's long bare back. Of course his cock was up like a hammer and he felt like an annoying horndog rubbing his cockhead against her silky ass like that, but that was life.

Last night he hadn't dared touch her. She had just been assaulted by some loony tunes redneck straight out of one of those shows about the swamps she had told him she loved. Ronnie Dobbs didn't have a long, gritty beard, but he was clearly unhinged enough to do some serious damage. Steffen couldn't afford to rule out murder as well. He'd talked to Tony Pickett last night. Tony had failed to apprehend Ronnie. It sounded as though Ronnie had lost Tony by going off-road in his souped-up truck with the monster tires.

Filtered light illuminated the master bedroom from the windows that crowned three of the room's walls. Steffen pinched the sheet and lifted it to see the beautiful slope of Willow's back. That was a telling curve, the waist flaring out to the rise of the hip like a sensuous snowy ridge. She had a strong character, this woman Steffen was in love with. Seeming halfway asleep, she arched her back erotically, stretching her legs, pointing her toes under the sheet. Steffen didn't like to leave the air conditioning on all night so they'd slept with just a sheet draped over them. Now he couldn't resist rubbing his erection against her ass. He couldn't tell if she was fully awake when she gyrated her ass against him, but like any man, he'd take anything he could get.

Then, one little wriggle, and his cock had slid halfway up Willow's cunt. He wanted to *swear* he hadn't done that on purpose, but if Willow was still half-asleep, he didn't want to wake her. Then again, would taking advantage of a sleeping woman constitute necrophilia, even though she was his girlfriend? Slinging one thigh slightly over her hip, he gave a little lunge of his hips, jarring her awake.

"Mm," she said.

What did that mean? Did that mean yes, or no? Stop, or go? Steffen lunged again, nudging his bursting cock even farther inside Willow. "Willow," he whispered.

"Mm?"

Assured she was truly awake and he wasn't being some zombie-loving deviant, Steffen gave a good swivel and drove his cock in deeply. Willow arched her back higher, offering herself up to him. *Ah.* It felt so good to be seated this deeply inside her. Steffen nearly came just from the swell of rapture that swirled around his balls and ran up his cock into his abdomen. He had to hold himself still for a few moments, lifting Willow's curtain of silky hair and biting the nape of her neck. She giggled. His cock twitched inside her, and she clenched her inner muscles around him, massaging his cock and making him gasp.

"Willow," he murmured, although he didn't know what he wanted to say. "My little filly."

She lazily raised herself on her knees and elbows. Steffen couldn't see her face, but it seemed that she wanted to be taken dogstyle. Steffen kneeled, clamping both thighs around hers. "You like this," he assumed.

"Mmm-hmm." Her pussy muscles clutched at his cock. She was strong, as though she'd been doing kegel exercises. Maybe the Ben Wa balls *did* help. "Horsy Style."

Steffen thought that was one of the Sunset Palomino Ranch menu items. He knew he wouldn't last long, so he just threw his all into seven, eight huge swinging lunges that had the woman gasping for breath and clutching the pillow. He erupted inside her heat, splashing her cervix with his seed.

He held himself deep inside her for a long time, relishing the way her inner pussy massaged and clutched at his prick. A shudder raced up and down his spine, jerking his cock seated deeply near her womb. On hands and knees, Willow swiveled her hips to give Steffen access to every possible angle. Finally she slumped, exhaling loudly, letting her head hang loosely. This was Steffen's sign. When he withdrew, she collapsed on her stomach hugging the pillow.

Her shoulders heaved, sending a stab of fear into Steffen's chest. Was she crying? But the few sounds that escaped from her were definitely laughs. Now he was relieved.

"Was that…" He realized he sounded corny. "Good?" *Who the hell asks that?*

She rolled onto her back, her tits jiggling like water balloons. Her face was adorably puffy from her deep sleep—and what Steffen hoped was a good fuck. "Of *course*, silly. I wouldn't let you take me if it wasn't."

He realized that once again, they'd done it without condoms. "You have to stop letting me do this, Willow. I'm so sorry I just jumped on you without a rubber."

Willow made a face and imitated an equally moronic guy. "'Oh, I'm so sorry. My penis just slipped inside you.' Don't worry, you gorgeous stud. I'm infertile. End of subject. If I was more worried I'd be using a sponge or whatever they use these days."

This brought up something that Steffen had been mulling since yesterday's adventure, after Willow had confessed to the miscarriage. Her infertility saddened him. He wondered why. It took him several hours of tossing it around in his mind to figure out why. *He wanted a child, too.* And with her.

But of course he hadn't known her that long, so he didn't dare bring it up in that manner. Now he said tentatively, "Are you completely certain about that? That you're infertile? Because that would be a shame."

She shrugged. She looked like a veritable Venus lying back like that, one arm above her head. "I've gotten used to the idea. I'm thirty-two. I'll be forty before I find anyone suitable to marry and be a father, anyway. By then it's too late. I keep reading articles, you know. So many women postponed children in favor of careers. They're only just now realizing you really can't do that. Your chances of getting pregnant are cut in half every year you age, or something like that. No. I have to look on the bright side of being childless. All my time is my own, all my money is my own. Well, the money I *hope* to have, anyway, once the motel opens for business."

With that, Willow wrenched herself from the bed and padded to the bathroom.

Steffen thought as he dressed. She obviously didn't see him as potential husband material. He had to feel her out He had to find out if it had even entered her mind that he might be a good husband.

So when she emerged from the bathroom and rooted around on the chair and ottoman for her clothes, Steffen asked casually, "Why would it take you another eight years to find a decent husband?"

She stepped into her panties. Since Dobbs was still at large, Steffen hadn't allowed her to go back to the *Ocean's 11* Room the night before, not even to get fresh clothes. He had hustled her into his truck and made a beeline for his house. "Oh, I don't know. I'm just very skeptical, as you can understand, having just gotten out of a horrible marriage. I didn't tell you. When Ronnie busted into my office last night, I was reading my final divorce papers. Yep. They came snail."

That little fact cheered Steffen up. "That's excellent, Willow. Now you're truly a free woman."

She pulled her strappy dress down over her head and smirked. "Yep. Free as a bird."

Steffen came closer. "I didn't mean that. Of course you're not 'free' as long as you're involved with me and Amadeo. Or Amadeo, or me separately." He frowned, serious. "You *do* realize that, don't you? I'm not going to take too kindly to coming into the Gadabout Cottage to see you with another man, you understand?"

He couldn't decipher her smile. But she looked down at his feet shyly. "I understand. I'm only allowed to mess around with you or Amadeo."

"Right. I mean, no! I mean, yes. That sounds about right. Does that bother you?"

She looked up, and a slow smile spread over her face. "No. Doesn't bother me at all. I kind of like it. Jealousy means that you like me."

Steffen scoffed and rolled his eyes at the ceiling. "I *more* than 'like' you, Willow." He didn't want to scare her away with any sappy declarations, yet he wanted her to know his intentions and rules.

"Do you 'more than like' Amadeo?"

Steffen hesitated. He'd been having the time of his life with both Willow and Amadeo, but how far could a threesome like that go? Steffen knew he wanted to be Willow's prime, main man, so how long before Amadeo felt like a third wheel and moved on? "Yes. I more than like him, too, but in a different way. I guess my feelings for you are…romantic. I don't feel nearly as flowery about Amadeo, but I think I'd be just as devastated if we had to stop seeing each other."

Willow nodded. "So it's a manlier sort of love."

Steffen nodded with relief. Willow had used the word, not him. "Exactly. I love him in a manlier, maybe a more practical way."

Willow's lower lip stuck out as she soaked up the information. "Good. Because I love him, too. Now, you're going to have to let me get back to the Searchlight, Steffen. I'll be perfectly safe there with Carl and all the workers around me. Even though it's Saturday I don't expect you to hang around with me, either. You must have a zillion things to do, as does Amadeo. I know he hasn't overseen all that hay-cutting that his hands are doing, and he said they need to keep the cattle moving to greener pastures. I'm not used to things drying out in Florida, but I guess his cattle have eaten all the grass up." She breezed back into the bathroom with her purse. She left the door open, so he guessed she was fixing her face.

He spoke to her from the bedroom. "I've been wanting to get over to his ranch, to take a look at his house again. I've been in it several times, talking to his father. I do recall it was a great piece of mid-century styling, with post and beam construction."

"Like yours?"

Steffen was impressed that Willow knew this. "Right. Only his is about four times as big as mine. This here is only eleven hundred square feet. Amadeo's house is built around boulders and palms, like the Kupka House."

"Yours is cute. It's got such an airy feeling, the way the interior walls don't go all the way to the ceilings. How the rooflines are slanted."

"Three-quarter walls. I like it, but I'm not particularly attached to it." Steffen had calculated this beforehand. He knew that if they could or wanted to make it work, the three of them, he'd move to the Lone Palm Ranch in a hot second. Amadeo's house was a stylish oasis that would be winning awards if it wasn't owned by an irascible, old-fashioned cowboy.

"Are you kidding?" Willow appeared in the bathroom doorway with a mascara wand in her hand. "Not attached to it? Steffen, you've put your *all* into this place! Why, that Steve Reiner dining set alone is to die for. And all the original fixtures in such good condition! The exposed beams, the butterfly roofline, the swimming pool, and don't get me started on those David Smock lamps in your living room!"

Steffen puffed with pride, not only that he owned David Smock lamps, but that Willow knew what they were. He wasn't a complete purist about his décor like so many were in the Modern Committee. He had a flat screen TV, modern appliances, and he had added solar panels and decent insulation. "Well. It's not really family-oriented with only eleven hundred square feet. Most kids want their own room."

He hadn't envisioned the response Willow would have to this innocent and estimable declaration. Her face fell like a shriveled apple and she looked almost about to cry. "Children, right…"

Dear Lord, how did he manage to blow so many things? Of course Willow would be upset that he wanted children. If she really couldn't have children, he must not be referring to her as his future wife! He raced to rectify the situation. "I mean adopted children, of course. You must have thought about that?"

Her wrinkly face smoothed out, and she nodded. "Oh. Right. Adopted. Of course it's occurred to me. So…you were thinking about living with me? Here?"

Steffen grinned. "Of course it's occurred to me." But he didn't want to press the point or get too heavy. "Come on. Let me take you back to the Searchlight. I've got to go inspect some crap that your socks-and-sandals friend has probably messed up in Rancho Mirage, but then I'll be back at the Searchlight keeping an eye on you."

However, as he was locking his front door behind him, it was Willow who brought up the subject again. "Do you really think Amadeo will want to keep playing with us if he's not allowed to fuck me? He *is* bi, you know."

"And you're one voluptuous filly. Yeah, I suppose he'll get frustrated eventually if I set too many hard limits on him. He's one hell of a Dom. I suppose I'll have to get over it eventually. I can't say I'll like watching it, but ideally I'll get used to it."

Willow grinned at him, standing by the passenger door of his truck. "Good. Because you know I love him just as I love you. Differently, but just as strongly. Like you said. It's more romantic with you. With Amadeo, it's more down to earth."

A swell of love rushed through Steffen's chest. "Good. My love for you is more romantic, that's for sure. I'd never get Amadeo flowers, for example."

"You've never given *me* flowers."

"Wait half an hour and that'll change. Get in the truck."

Chapter Thirteen

Amadeo was surprised to find the door of the Gadabout Cottage wide open. He'd already seen Carl working on the Atomic Café's outdoor lighting and palm thatch roof, so who was lurking around *their* private cottage?

He hadn't read the text from the cops until this morning. He'd been up since four with some hands fixing fences, so he didn't read about Ronnie Dobbs's truck being seen in front of the Searchlight until around ten. Of course then he'd leaped in his truck and zoomed to the motel—neither Willow nor Steffen were answering their cells.

After Willow had vanished yesterday, Amadeo had gone back to ranching duties. He had no desire to visit the Racquet Club anymore. Why would he, when he had two play partners as good as any in that kink community? He was passionate about Steffen of course—had been for decades—and he hadn't felt this aroused over another women for years. Willow was shapely, with a serenity about her that was necessary to run such an extensive motel operation. Things wouldn't freak her out, like birthing lambs or having to shoot a coyote that was killing your stock.

He realized he was already thinking of his two lovers in long-term ways. Steffen would get over his jealousy once he relaxed and started trusting Amadeo more. Amadeo knew how he would display to Steffen that he was trustworthy. His devious plans had to do with the St. Andrew's Cross they hadn't made use of yet. If he would volunteer to be shackled to the cross at Steffen's beck and call, Steffen would learn to trust him. It was a perfect plan.

Amadeo approached the cottage warily, his hand on the pistol in his hip holster. He had decided to pack even when he wasn't on his ranch, thanks to that doofus Ronnie Dobbs running around stalking Willow for a stupid wristwatch. Peeking around the corner of the cottage's door, Amadeo saw a blonde fellow in filthy jeans with a tool belt on. His back was to Amadeo as he fussed around with something near the St. Andrew's Cross. Amadeo drew the pistol and cocked the hammer.

"Who the fuck are you?"

The fellow twirled around, a look of complete horror on his face. He had one of those beet-red faces that looked to be caused by skiing but was probably due to acute alcoholism, drugs, or both. The guy held up his hands as though accustomed to being arrested, and came toward Amadeo. "Chas White, the contractor here, El Mirador Construction. I was just checking on the, uh, the—"

Amadeo holstered his weapon. "Never mind. I know who you are. Just never *seen* you before. I'm Amadeo Barbieri of—"

"Lone Palm Ranch, right! Right, right, I've been meaning to meet with you about that punch list for the tack room. I had some great ideas. You know how the ceiling joists—"

Drugs *and* alcohol were responsible for Chas White's shoddy work as well as his face. His teeth had that rotten, twisted characteristic of the chronic meth-head. "That's fine." Amadeo interrupted Chas because Steffen and Willow were coming down the pathway. "Look, I've got to talk to my friends about some urgent matters. Will you be answering your cell in, say, two hours?"

"Sure will! Miss Paige wanted to talk about something with me, too—oh!"

When Miss Paige saw Amadeo she broke into a run, dropping the enormous bag she always carried on one shoulder. She flung her arms around his neck as though she hadn't seen him in a month, peppering his mouth with little kisses. She pushed him into the cottage, Steffen presumably following, because Amadeo heard someone slam the door.

"Oh, Amadeo, I missed you so much!"

Amadeo held her wrists and drew back to examine her. Was she doing some of Chas White's drugs? "I'm so glad you're fine, Willow! I'm so fucking sorry I didn't get out here sooner, but I didn't get Officer Tony's text until ten this morning. My bad. I didn't mean to throw you under the bus, honestly, I didn't."

Willow seemed happy enough. "It's all right. Steffen here was manly and saved me. And Officer Tony, too, of course."

"Okay," said Amadeo. "But Dobbs is still at large. Tell me exactly what happened with Dobbs."

So they sat on the burnt orange couches and explained what Dobbs had done. Willow had a bandage on her neck where Dobbs had cut her, so they explained how he'd gagged her and was walking her to the cottage. She had hoped to pawn off a generic leather wrist cuff on him because he didn't seem to know exactly what he was looking for.

Willow said, "Not after rambling on about Scott Baio's paper towel holder and Erik Estrada's socks."

"That's off the hook!" cried Amadeo. "How the hell would anyone *believe* any socks belonged to Erik Estrada?"

"Exactly!" said Willow. "Dobbs is just a shitastic turkey, that's all."

"And a David Soul album?" Amadeo wrinkled his face with disbelief. "That probably goes for about ten bucks on eBay. Ridiculous!"

"The guy is one sandwich short of a picnic," Steffen agreed. "But how do we keep Willow safe while he's off the grid? I talked to Tony just now. No Dobbs at his house in Beaumont, of course. They've got the place staked out, but he's smart enough not to go home."

"Right," said Amadeo. "I think it's just a matter of time before he does some new asinine thing, like kill himself while deep-frying a frozen turkey."

"Or climbing into a wine fermentation vat to get drunk," Willow added.

Amadeo stood and held out his hands. He was in control of the situation. "Listen. I'm a cowboy. I'm going to pack this gun no matter where I go, you hear? And I'm not leaving your fucking side until Dobbs is caught. I can help Carl or Chas or whoever's working on the Atomic Café so I'm not completely useless. I've got plenty of hands at the ranch to fix fences and move the cattle to other pastures. I see you've got a pistol, too, Steffen. Good."

"Yeah, no shit," agreed Steffen. "I doubt Dobbs could get any firearms legally with such an extensive record, but you never know. The black market abounds with them, and any criminal can get one."

Amadeo locked the cottage door and let down a blind. It looked as though all the blinds had been hung, and the horizontal slats of sun streaming onto the carpet did give the room a fifties ambiance. "For now, I've got a plan. A plan I think might help you trust me more, Steffen."

Steffen said, "You mean trust you around my girlfriend."

"Exactly. I'm going to let *you* shackle me to that St. Andrew's Cross. Have your way with me. My wrists will be shackled, so I can't touch Willow. You can let us get as close as you want, or not. Here. I found this the other day." He handed Steffen a finely sanded wooden paddle he'd found in the Cesar Romero Room. He had stashed it in one of the cottage's kitchen drawers, safe from Ronnie Dobbs and his penchant for bondage memorabilia. He stripped off his shirt and white wifebeater because he knew his hairless chest turned on both Steffen and Willow. She was sitting on her feet on the couch, having kicked off her shoes, and her eyes shined with excitement.

"Okay. Buckle me in." Amadeo stood on the footboard of the cross, fitting his wrists into the suspension cuffs someone had been kind enough to bolt to the cross.

"But your shoes are on," Willow complained. "As macho as I think cowboy boots look."

"That's okay. You want to see me in my chaps, don't you?"

Steffen answered quickly as he buckled Amadeo's wrists, "Of course. Nothing more stimulating than a stud muffin cowboy naked except for boots and chaps."

"Ooh, I've got an idea." Having finished cinching his ankles, Willow went to the kitchenette and came back with a bottle of olive oil. She hesitated, though, looking at his naked torso. "Steffen. May I?"

Steffen had to think about it for a few seconds. He nodded to Willow. He could only do a couple of things at once, and oiling up Amadeo's torso wasn't one of them.

"Ooh, yes," she said excitedly as she dribbled a line of oil across his pecs. Her hand felt heavenly as she rubbed his smooth chest. She didn't ignore his armpits, where he was a bit ticklish, and her oily hand followed the line of hair that arrowed toward his pubic bone. That was when Steffen snatched her hand away. He wanted to unbuckle the belt himself.

That he had left one of the blinds only halfway closed gave Amadeo an extra thrill. He'd always been a bit of an exhibitionist. He knew he was a great strapping caveman of a stud that both men and women loved to ogle, and already a few of Chas's workers were peeking into the window, squinting as if to make sure they weren't hallucinating.

Steffen pretended not to notice as he slid a palm down the front of Amadeo's jeans and grabbed a handful of cock. "Are you always hard?" he asked good-naturedly. "Your long, juicy cock seems to always be hard. Willow, drizzle some oil on this dick."

Willow did as commanded, and soon Steffen was jacking the whole length of Amadeo's dick with the oil, greasing up his testicles the size of tennis balls. He seemed to take great enjoyment in slowly arousing Amadeo, obviously turned on by the visual of his hand squeezing the slick meat. Or maybe he was stimulated by watching his girlfriend tweak Amadeo's pebbled nipples, harshly rubbing her fingertips in a circular motion around the nipples, and how that made Amadeo's dick twitch and jump.

Once he'd gotten Amadeo's penis nice and oiled, Steffen smacked it with the paddle. Amadeo's whole body twitched. Instinctively he squeezed his eyes shut. It had been a long time since he'd felt the sudden pain-pleasure of cock-and-ball torture, but Steffen seemed to be a natural. As Willow's little hand moved around to slide his jeans down and oil up his ass, swirling her fingertips around his tense asshole, Steffen expertly spanked his greasy cock with the paddle as though he'd been born to it. Maybe he'd seen it done at the Racquet Club—Amadeo hoped. Thinking of Steffen playing with other men riddled his stomach with jealousy too, and he understood how Steffen might feel, watching Amadeo touch his girlfriend.

"You think you're just a big stud," snarled Steffen. *Slap*. "You think just everyone wants to get a piece of you because you're so built and carved." *Smack.* "Well, this is your punishment." *Slap.*

Amadeo looked up from under his lashes. "Except I like it. Every time you spank my cock it gets bigger."

"That's true." *Smack.* In between slaps, Steffen caressed the cock lovingly, his nostrils flaring, his iceberg blue eyes looking down his nose at the bound man. The only movement Amadeo could make was to thrust his hips toward Steffen, to display his pleasure, that he wanted more, more. *Slap*. "You're being even badder than I thought. This is actually arousing you, having your dick paddled."

"Try this." Willow's voice came from behind Amadeo, and he only saw her arm stretching out to offer something to Steffen.

Steffen's evil grin told Amadeo what he needed to know. "A cock ring. Nice touch, Willow."

Steffen said, "Not just any cock ring. Cock *bling*. This thing is studded with rhinestones."

Willow said, "It was just hanging over the arm of this cross. Looks clean."

It was the sort of black leather ring that would go below the balls, scrunching them up and making them appear more prominent. Steffen cinched it around the ball sac with a flourish. His own package was bulging the crotch of his jeans, and he seemed to like the look of the eager, stimulated cock and balls being squeezed like that. If Amadeo pretended to struggle against his bonds, all that jerked was his bound cock and balls, bobbing in the air all greased up, and Steffen stepped back with crossed arms to admire his handiwork.

"Let me go, you damned bastard," Amadeo pretended to protest.

Steffen stepped up to dribble more oil on the cock. "Not on your life. You're our prisoner now, our slave." He bent to clamp his mouth over one of Amadeo's nipples. His nibbling sent pangs of painful ecstasy shooting down Amadeo's abdomen directly into his cock. Willow dared to bend and slurp at the other nipple. Steffen didn't seem to mind that. Maybe Amadeo was making some headway.

Steffen backed away again. "Hold the cock up," he commanded Willow. They shared a conspiratorial look, and Amadeo knew what was coming.

Smack. The entire scrunched-up ball sac was paddled, and finally Amadeo let out a strangled yell. *That did hurt*. But no matter how many times Steffen paddled his poor scrunched-up sac, the cock just grew in Willow's hand. The men at the window—there now appeared to be a woman as well—were getting handprints and noseprints all over the glass with their drooling. A couple of the workers were even massaging their own erections through their pants, and Amadeo was proud to be the cause of their ardor.

"You like those people watching you torture my cock and balls," Amadeo growled between spankings.

Swat. Steffen's features were lopsided, drunk with power. Amadeo had seen this effect many times in Doms high on the endorphin rush of dominance. "I like how it's turning them on watching your big, swollen cock get paddled."

"Do you trust me now?" Amadeo asked between gritted teeth.

"Oh, I trust you all right. I always did, Amadeo. I just wanted to get you into a helpless position so you have no say in what I do." Tossing the paddle onto a couch, Steffen put a hand on Willow's shoulder. "Get on your knees and pleasure him. But not too fast. I want to get my pleasure of him, too."

And Steffen walked around the back of the cross. Amadeo could hear him unbuckling his belt, then the rounded nudging of Steffen's delicious cockhead at the wrinkled opening to his anus. "Oh, that's good," Amadeo murmured, wiggling his ass to encourage Steffen. "Good. Fuck me like I'm a girl. Show me what a man you are. I want to feel your dick driving all the way up my ass."

Steffen slapped the oily ass loudly with a cupped hand. "I'll teach you to keep your mouth shut, or I won't give you a nice hard fucking. Willow. Is his prick tasty? Can you swallow all of it?"

"Not all," Willow admitted, but she was doing a damn fine job. "I think I have a small mouth compared to most women."

"Get back on it," Amadeo gasped.

Steffen swatted Amadeo's ass. "Shut the fuck up or I'll gag you. You don't think I'll use that ball gag we found? You think I'm too submissive for that?"

Amadeo half-laughed and half-groaned. "I don't think so at all."

"That's good." Steffen encouraged Willow to deep-throat Amadeo. She took his cockhead farther and farther back into her throat, but Amadeo knew she would choke. She *did* have a small, pouty mouth, but she was working it like mad, filling Amadeo with nearly painful lust—and also pride.

Steffen was including him. Amadeo wasn't on the outside looking in. He was sandwiched—spit roasted—between his two lovers, being reamed up the ass by the biggest, most muscular cock he'd seen in and out of the Racquet Club, while being sucked by the shapely Miss Paige. *What does Steffen call her? Sublime. She's a sublime sub.*

"Oh, *God!*" Steffen continued swatting Amadeo's ass cheek loud, leaving a pleasant sting that radiated down his thighs. He reached around and got a handful of Amadeo's testicles, full and bulging in the stricture of the cock ring. "Nice tight ass…driving me crazy…Get him off, Willow, while I pound his nice tight ass."

When Steffen hit Amadeo's prostate gland and gyrated his hips like a stripper, massaging it exquisitely, Amadeo went off like a rocket. His entire body twitched and shuddered like someone being beamed onto an alien craft. Willow's talented little mouth suckled and drew the seed from him while Steffen held his dick deep inside Amadeo, twitching with his own orgasmic spasms. Although unfamiliar with humping other men, Steffen milked Amadeo's prostate efficiently, his cockhead kneading and stroking the spot that gave Amadeo so much ecstasy.

"Whoa!" Willow was the first to withdraw, falling back onto her butt on the carpet. Amadeo panted and laughed down at her. She looked like a roller skater on her butt with that flippy little skirt spread out. Leaning back on her hands, she looked up at the two men with shining eyes. "Never seen such an amazing sight in my life."

"Neither have they," Steffen panted, and Amadeo knew he meant the appreciative audience at the window.

Amadeo was pleasantly surprised to see that their performance had spurred at least two men to ejaculate against the window. *Who cares? They're the ones going to have to clean it.* The woman outside had completely vanished, presumably to finish the job with one of the men, and hopefully in a more private atmosphere. "We can't be doing this once the motel's open," Amadeo noted.

Willow shrugged. "Not unless we charge extra for a matinee. Right?"

Steffen's laughter assisted his cock to slide from Amadeo's ass, and he continued laughing as he unbuckled one of Amadeo's cuffs. "Here, Willow. Get the other one. Yeah, I've often found it to be exciting, exhibiting myself for people. But I can understand if Miss Paige doesn't want to. I don't really want any strangers looking at her. Right, Amadeo?"

"Right," Amadeo agreed. Experimentally he lowered his arms. He expected them to be sort of numb from the blood rushing from his hands, and they were. Willow, unbuckling an ankle shackle, rose to lick Amadeo's cock that hung like a dead rubber hose, dangling down his thigh. He nearly shot through the ceiling at the sudden shock of sensation. "Girl! Back down!"

Steffen counseled his girlfriend. "Remember we tried to give you aftercare after the ride on the pool table? Let's go easy on Amadeo. Go make him a gimlet and there should be some chocolate there on the wet bar."

"I prefer a regular manly whiskey," said Amadeo, bending to massage his ankles. He walked to the window and yanked the blinds to drop them even though one fellow was still eagerly jerking his pole. "What should we call that menu item?"

"Hot Cross Buns," Steffen said instantly.

"Hey, you're good at that," said Willow at the wet bar, where she was unscrewing a bottle of whiskey. "Making up menu items. Hot Cross Buns, of course, is an appetizer. I was thinking of framing that original Sunset Palomino menu that I found, what do you think? We could either put it up here in the cottage, or in the lob—"

A sharp, loud bang sounded out. At first, Amadeo was just in shock, looking around the room. Whatever it was had come through the open window where he'd just lowered the blinds. Glass had exploded inward, carpeting one of the burnt orange couches. Was someone pissed off that he'd closed the blind and had thrown something through the window? Amadeo thrust a straight arm at Willow. “Down!” he commanded, and she crouched behind the bar as he withdrew his pistol.

“You got yours?” he shouted at Steffen, but Steffen was one step ahead of him. The building inspector peeked around the other side of the window, holding the blinds apart with his fingers like in a spaghetti western. The barrel of his pistol faced the ceiling, as did Amadeo’s. Workers outside milled around in confusion, although it sounded as though most of them swiftly departed the immediate area.

“It sounded like a gun!” yelled one worker.

“But where did it come from?” shouted another.

Amadeo said, “I heard no report coming from outside. Where did the bullet hit? *Don’t move, Willow!*”

“I want to help,” Willow whispered from behind the wet bar.

“Look,” said Steffen. “The wall over there. My poster of Liberace, the glass is shattered.”

Amadeo said, “Looks like a…*an arrow* sticking out from it? You stay here. Keep an eye out, see if you can see the shooter. I’m checking out Liberace.”

Indeed, an arrow shaft was buried about three inches in the drywall. Amadeo was hesitant but really had no choice other than to pull it out, gingerly as though the shaft itself would explode. He took his ever-present Swiss army knife from his pocket and dug around in the hole in the wall.

“Be careful,” said Steffen needlessly. “A plain arrow doesn’t make a sound like that.”

Sure enough, Amadeo dug out a bullet casing, what looked like a .38 or .357 Magnum round. “This asshole somehow managed to encase a round into some kind of plastic cylinder, and shoot it through this window.”

“I’ve already dialed 911,” said Willow.

Steffen said, “Well, I ain’t waiting for those cops to dick around again. We know who it is. He’s out there somewhere with a fucking compound bow, and we've got pistols." Steffen broke away from the window and joined Amadeo by the shattered Liberace poster. "Judging from this trajectory, he's down by the pétanque court."

Willow peeked around the corner of the wet bar. "He'd be stupid if he's still there," she pointed out. Into her phone she said, "Yes, I'd like to report a, uh, a shooting at the Searchlight Motel on Manilow Avenue."

"Come on." Steffen lifted his chin at Amadeo. "We're getting this motherfucker once and for all."

Chapter Fourteen

Willow wasn't about to sit around like a lame duck waiting for the next shot, or arrow, or whatever the hell Ronnie Dobbs was using to shoot at Liberace's poster. Her two men were already out the door and heading down the lawn toward the pétanque court like two shirtless demigods.

Luckily her dress had pockets, so Willow slid her cell into one and the "cock bling" into another. She'd never seen this bedazzled cock ring before today, and it did look as though it might be a cuff, too. If she could somehow give it to Ronnie as an offering maybe he'd back off long enough to experience his final—or one of his final—arrests.

She saw just a flash of Steffen's and Amadeo's feet as they sprinted around the corner of a breezeway. She halted briefly when she noted Carl cowering behind an enormous planter. "Carl!" She didn't try to drag him out from his hiding place, but he sure tried to drag her in.

"What the fuck?" he shrieked in a high-pitched voice. "I didn't hear no gun go off, but suddenly your window was shattered and it sure sounded like something exploding inside the cottage!"

"Yeah, it's Ronnie Dobbs again, of course. He didn't nail anyone, just the Liberace poster." She heard a lot of shouting coming from the pétanque court area. "He's got some kind of bow that can shoot bullets that I guess only explode on impact. Did you notice which direction it came from? Down there by the pétanque court?"

Carl's eyes were bugged out. "Yeah, but you don't be going down there, Miss Paige, hear? Those two big guys of yours went running past with guns. I'm shaking like a dog shitting razor blades. They'll never forgive me if I let you run down there. Wait for the cops!"

Another sharp explosion had Willow's eyes bugging out too, and they both stared in the direction of the ball court. Other than that, all was dead quiet on the motel's grounds, the other workers having taken cover like Carl. Willow thought she heard Ronnie Dobb's frenzied drawl screeching some shit, so she darted down the lawn, too.

"You be careful, Miss Paige!" shrieked Carl before hiding behind the potted palm again.

Once she got closer, she could hear what Dobbs was bellowing about. He actually didn't seem to be directing his tirade at Steffen or Amadeo. There seemed to be a third person he was angry with. She listened from behind the protection of the building.

"You think you can lecture me? Well you've got another thing coming! I wasn't here to *steal* you—I was here to help you move forward into a new phase in your life!"

Say what? Willow dared to peek around the corner. Sure enough, Ronnie Dobbs, back to resembling Bart Simpson's bus driver with his long pyramidal black wedge hairdo, was waving a compound bow around. A quiver with a few arrows was mounted to the bow, and it looked as though one was already nocked and ready to draw as Ronnie waved the bow around. Who was he yelling at?

Not at her two men. They stood with pistols dangling at their sides, looking equally dumbfounded as Ronnie yelled at…a *cactus*? *Holy shit!* It looked as though Ronnie had been shooting at one of Willow's giant beloved saguaro cacti! Those cacti had cost her a fortune! She had planted six of them in a row to showcase the lovely valley beyond at the foot of the San Jacinto Mountains—the valley where one could see parts of Amadeo's ranch. What was this fucktard doing shooting arms off her cacti? A hundred year's of nature's work lay splattered on the ground, and for what? A shovel was stuck into the earth at the base of the twenty-foot tall cactus as though Ronnie had started digging, but apparently the cactus was getting the better of him.

"I'm sick of your lecturing!" Ronnie cried, pointing an accusing finger at the saguaro. "I haven't done wrong! *You* have done wrong! I've got no sins to pay for! *You're* the one disturbing the cactus universe!"

Steffen and Amadeo shared haunted looks. Amadeo first raised his pistol slowly at Ronnie. "Ronnie Dobbs! Throw down your bow!" Meanwhile, Steffen circled around to flank Ronnie and gain better coverage if they needed to pick him off.

Ronnie twirled with the bow to face Amadeo. He looked confused at first, but realization dawned on his face. "You! You're that he-man always boinking Willow Paige!"

"I said *put down the bow!"* Amadeo repeated. Willow was impressed with how his arm holding the pistol didn't waver the tiniest bit, aimed directly at Ronnie's head. She had never had any gun training, but she supposed it was foolhardy to point a weapon at anyone unless you intended to use it. *Amadeo must intend to use it.*

Ronnie didn't put down the bow. He pointed his free arm at the offending cactus. "This here cactus is trying to tell me I'm going to pay for stealing it! But I was only trying to help!"

"Help by shooting through the cottage window?" shouted Steffen.

Ronnie pivoted about on one foot, looking first at Steffen, then Amadeo, then the cactus, then back to Steffen. He seemed unsure as to who was his biggest, most threatening enemy. "What cottage window?"

Steffen yelled, "The one you just shot that bullet-arrow through!"

Ronnie pointed at the cactus. "The cactus was coming to get me! I'd do it again in a heartbeat the second it starts coming after—*Agh!"* Twirling about, Ronnie gaped at the looming saguaro. It had looked very noble and majestic silhouetted against the valley floor before ole Ronnie had shot its arm off. Now, it *did* sort of look pissed-off and threatening, Willow had to admit that much. "No, *you* are!" Ronnie yelled at the cactus. "*You're* the one disturbing the cactus universe! For that you must pay!" And he raised the bow again to shoot the poor harmless cactus.

Surprisingly, it was Steffen who shot the bow out of Ronnie's hands. It was whipped out of Ronnie's hand, and dropped to the ground.

Ronnie didn't seem to notice it was Steffen who shot the bow. He looked in surprise at his splayed hands as though they were bombs that had exploded, then back to the cactus with round cartoonish eyes. "Oh, saguaro!" he wailed. "You've been a menace to the west my entire life! And they tried calling *me* the menace to the west! Saguaro, O saguaro! Show me the true path!"

And he ran headlong into the giant dinosaur of a cactus, arms open as if to welcome it into his bosom.

Willow was the first to rush over to the saguaro. Amadeo and Steffen appeared rooted to the spot, amazed. She was just in time to see that some long cactus needles had stabbed Ronnie in the eyes and face. He appeared quite content as he hugged the body of the saguaro, his rubbery mouth turned up in a blissful smile, and only the feeblest trickle of breath seemed to come from him.

"Willow!" yelled Steffen, suddenly at her elbow. "Get away! You don't need to see that! That douche bag got what he deserved." He tore her from the scene, hauling her back up the hill toward the wing of the motel she'd been hiding behind. They passed by the sprinting Amadeo, who jogged toward the cactus.

She protested, "But Steffen, those cactus needles are long, maybe two inches. It looks like he jammed some through his face!"

Steffen held her firmly with her back against the building. His natural oaky scent surrounded her, calmed her. Workers were starting to tiptoe down the hill to see what had transpired. "He would've done the same to you, filly."

"Holy shit!" cried a worker. "He's glued to the cactus!"

Willow had to remember how he'd gagged her and cut her throat. Not to mention how he'd shot at them through the window of the Gadabout Cottage. "I know. You're right, Steffen. We'll just let the paramedics take care of him. I was going to hand him this just to get him to shut up and go away, but now I guess we'll never know why he wanted that artifact so badly. I was going to pretend it was what he was looking for. He didn't seem too sure about what he really wanted."

"The cock ring? Hell, Ronnie Dobbs didn't seem too sure about *anything*, Willow. He's crazier than a soup sandwich. Did you hear how he was ranting at the cactus like it was alive, like it was tormenting him?"

Willow wanted to laugh and cry at the same time. "I couldn't figure out if he thought the cactus was his father, or it was alive, coming to get him."

"He *was* trying to steal it. I wouldn't blame it for being pissed off. Well, here come the cops. Let's get you somewhere safe, back up to your room or something."

They started walking against the flowing tide of cops that rushed belatedly down the hill just as Amadeo caught up to them.

"We won't need the paramedics," Amadeo told them. "He's gone. Some of those needles must've pierced his brain or something. He's just standing there completely impaled through and through, like an iron maiden. What's up with the cock ring?" Amadeo took it from Steffen.

Steffen said, "I'll bet it's a long time until anyone beats his record of being 'the most arrested man in the Coachella Valley.' Hey, Officer Tony. Amadeo here just told us Ronnie Dobbs is down there, expired."

Willow hoped one of them wouldn't be accused of doing the deed. She'd watched too many cop shows in her time. It would be a difficult story to believe, that Ronnie had run into the cactus himself. But the cops knew Ronnie well, so maybe it wouldn't be such a stretch.

Officer Tony didn't seem concerned with Ronnie. "You know what else is odd? Just half an hour ago a guy named Chas White was arrested going like a bat out of hell toward Beaumont with a stolen barrel cactus in the back of his truck. Got taken in for DUI, started raving about how he was in cahoots with Ronnie Dobbs, how they drank mescal and took some peyote so they could get all mystical and go steal some cacti they'd seen at the Searchlight ."

"Those things are valuable," Steffen agreed.

"Right. He said they became afraid when apparently the psychedelic properties started to sink into their brains and they imagined a giant saguaro they were trying to steal had come alive, so Chas White ran. He said he put something back into your cottage that he'd stolen because the giant cactus was lecturing him about it, and then he sped off into the desert. I found a box in Chas's truck that seems to match the one you said was stolen from one of your rooms. Silk-lined with two circular indentations inside."

"That's it. Hey," said Amadeo, holding up the cock ring. "It's funny how this showed up right after I busted Chas lurking around in the Gadabout Cottage, right before you came up." He turned it around, holding it up to the light, peering inside of it.

"That doesn't surprise me." Suddenly Carl Bogart was there, acting equally as confident and bold as ten minutes earlier he'd been cowering in terror. "I always knew Chas was a taco short of a combination plate. I'm telling you, once he showed up for work as drunk as a drag queen walking on a fence. He got stuck in the portable toilet because he couldn't figure out the handle and started yelling that we'd locked him in there. Finally he knocked it over from inside. Now, that's a sight you never want to see." Carl chuckled with the memory. "That's when we started calling them 'Port-a-Poppins.' Because Chas was thrashing around so wildly the thing was practically flying."

Steffen squeezed Willow with the arm he had like a vise around her shoulders. “Tony, if you don’t mind, I’m taking Willow back up to her room. Come get us when you need a statement.”

Carl said, “We all saw the whole thing. We can vouch that Dobbs is crazier than a dog in a hubcap factory, shooting at that poor cactus. He had some weird arrows that he fitted with heads that exploded like bullets. Shot out the cottage window, too, when these three were—ah, inside.”

Willow frowned. “Carl, I saw you. You were hiding behind that potted palm.”

Steffen gave her a little shake and began to drag her off. “Willow, he probably saw most of *everything*.”

“That’s right.” Willow remembered the blinds had been halfway up during their play session, so Carl could have seen a lot, indeed. She should not try to rile poor Carl, who was probably already traumatized by the day’s events.

“I’ll get your statements later,” said Tony casually as he started down the hill with Carl.

Willow heard Carl yammering at Officer Tony. “Once, there was an earthquake when we were out in Indio in a construction trailer. Both Chas and I tried to get through the same door at the same time. Course we got stuck. People were piling up behind us, pushing on us, starting to panic, but Chas wouldn’t relent. He kept trying to squish through the door, scared as a sinner in a cyclone. Man, talk about ignoring ‘women and children first.’ There was a pregnant secretary in the trailer!”

Tony said, “But *you* were trying to get through the door, too.”

Suddenly Willow was very tired. “I wonder what I’ll do about the cactus. I know it can be saved, but isn’t it kind of a morbid reminder of Ronnie?”

“It’ll be a tourist attraction,” Steffen suggested. “You don’t want to kill a hundred-year-old cactus just for the sake of one asshat.”

"That's true." Willow sighed. She leaned her head against Steffen's bare shoulder as they walked toward the lobby. "The cactus *did* save everyone from that 'menace to the west.' Kind of poetic justice that it lobotomized him."

"Hey, look at this," said Amadeo remotely as they entered the shelter of the breezeway. He returned out into the direct sunlight in order to squint at something on the inside of the leather cuff. "Something is engraved in here, stamped or etched or whatever you want to call it."

Willow looked up at Steffen. "Maybe Ronnie *did* know what he was looking for."

Amadeo read, "'My beloved Bobbie. Forever yours, Cesar. April 1960.'"

Willow's jaw dropped. "Cesar? How is it spelled? The usual way Caesar is spelled, as in Julius?"

Amadeo shook his head. "Nope. C-E-S-A-R."

Willow spoke in a hush. "That's how Cesar Romero spelled his name. Amadeo! Steffen! This *is* the memorabilia Ronnie was looking for! He was right for once!"

Steffen took the item from Amadeo. "Yeah, but…Cesar Romero's *cock ring*?"

Amadeo shrugged. "Maybe it's not a cock ring. It could easily fit on the wrist of a woman named Bobbie if you used the inside snaps. Short for Roberta."

Steffen said, "Or the cock of a *man* named Bobbie. Ronnie could have been trying to blackmail Romero's estate, to make money off exploiting something people might think was sordid."

"Whichever the case," said Willow, "*we're* not going to exploit it. I might put it in a display case, but where no one can see the inscription and without labeling it."

Steffen suggested, "Put it in a case next to your framed menu from the Sunset Palomino Ranch."

Willow tilted her head. "In the lobby or in the cottage?"

Steffen continued herding her toward the stairs that led to the *Ocean's 11* Room. "Come on. We can figure that out once we've got you all nice and safe."

But Willow already felt safe. She would always feel safe as long as she was between her two men. Suddenly she felt a glorious future open up in front of her, as supersonic and out of sight as the airy and light-filled architecture the three of them loved.

Or, as Steffen would say, sublime.

Epilogue

"The slate contractor just left," said Amadeo.

Restoration to the Sunset Palomino Ranch house was nearly complete. Amadeo posed next to the built-in barbecue looking like a James Bond figure in his Hawaiian shirt, holding a scotch on the rocks glass. In fact, the house *had* been used for a Bond movie decades ago, with bikini-clad vixens posing on the boulders the house was ingeniously built around. The house had been excavated out of natural boulders in the surrounding desert ridge, built by Amadeo's father. They had renamed Lone Palm Ranch as the Sunset Palomino Ranch to give kudos to the defunct bordello that had brought the three of them together. Willow, who had enthusiastically joined Steffen's Modern Committee, had convinced them to allow public tours of the one-of-a-kind house once refurbishment was complete.

Steffen executed some cool laps in the sixty-five-degree night air around the indoor-outdoor pool. The moveable glass partitions had been mechanically opened to the refreshing October desert air, so Steffen could stroke from the very edge of the pool, elevated thirty feet above the desert floor, to the other end. Here the gigantic UFO-like domed concrete roof that covered the circular living room also protected the indoor part of the pool, where Amadeo had apparently just made a drink at the wet bar.

"But the sealer isn't dry yet," Steffen assumed, treading water. The dramatic original black slate tiled floors had been cut around massive groups of boulders in the living room. But ages of cowboys treading dirt and shit across them had worn them dull, and the contractor had just polished and sealed them.

"No," confirmed Amadeo, striding over to the outdoor portion of the patio, luring Steffen to swim back over there with the. "We can't walk in there until the morning. We'll have to go through these sliders into the bedroom or the kitchen."

Amadeo didn't even resemble a cowboy anymore. He'd taken a more managerial role in the cattle ranching side of the business after his father had passed two months ago, thus the Hawaiian shirt and khaki slacks. Although of course he still wore jeans and chaps out on the range, Steffen liked this new look on him, and as he stroked naked through the warm, airy water, his dick got hard.

As Steffen rose from the water into the shallower part of the pool like a Bond actor, his hands dangled at his sides. He didn't care that the myriad of nighttime pool lights cast another myriad of enormous penis-shaped shadows all around the walls of the pool. Steffen was proud of his hard-on, proud of his lust and love for the virile cattle rancher. Everyone he worked with at City Hall knew he lived with a man and a woman. Even the ones who frowned upon it didn't dare to make that known anymore. Not in today's day and age.

Amadeo grinned that crooked grin as he sat on the edge of the steps. Already barefoot, he put his drink down and started to roll up his pants legs. But Steffen was in a feisty mood. Knocking Amadeo's knees apart with his hips, he took one knee in each hand and brushed his lips against Amadeo's full, bowed ones.

"I want you, you big, hunky thing," he snarled. "Only tonight, guess who's going to claim your ass?"

"You are?"

Steffen felt Amadeo grin against his mouth. More and more the past few months they had been switching. The game they'd played in the Gadabout Cottage the day Ronnie Dobbs had shot the arrow-bullet through the cottage window had lingered in Steffen's mind long after. Binding the robust stud until he was helpless, feeling the smack of his stiff flesh against his palm when Steffen whipped him, and drilling the tight, muscular ass until he accepted his gushing load, it had all taken Steffen by storm.

More and more often now, Amadeo was content to play the bottom, probably relishing being worshipped. Amadeo knew that the more compliant he seemed, the more power he actually wielded. The sight of a squirming, hairless, muscular stud begging to be oiled and reamed was a sight to arouse the dullest tool in the shed. All Amadeo had to do was to lift his arms and thread his fingers together at the back of his neck and Steffen was on him like a wolf, suckling his nipples, licking his underarms, and massaging his cock. Amadeo turned his head and submissively showed his bare throat and Steffen was on top of him, humping him madly. In a way, Amadeo had Steffen by the short hairs, though nominally, Steffen was now the Dom most of the time.

Steffen closed his mouth over Amadeo's in a bruising kiss. He adored making out with this Latin lover. He spiraled his tongue around Amadeo's, clutching him close by digging his fingers into the globes of his ass. Their stiff pricks rubbed together as they ground their hips against each other. "I'm going to drill you," Steffen murmured between sloppy kisses.

Amadeo smiled. "Take me," he growled in that low, resonant voice that never failed to send Steffen over the edge.

He detached with a loud smack of the lips, fixing Amadeo with his eyes, panting. "I love you. You know that, don't you?"

"Of course," Amadeo said, like a flirtatious teen. "I managed to seduce the quarterback. I'd say I'm doing pretty good for myself."

Steffen frowned and slapped the cock that poked out at him impudently. "Don't get so damned full of yourself!"

"Not until I'm full of *you*," Amadeo said.

It was both corny and brilliant at the same time, and all Steffen could do was slap the cock some more. He barely remembered Amadeo as the unruly musician who would rather toke on a bong than a big juicy cock. Now he'd buffed up, filled out, come into his own.

Steffen liked the ripe, mature Amadeo. He wouldn't have liked the guitar player in the plaid shirt—although Steffen did sometimes wish he had met Amadeo earlier in the dungeons of the Racquet Club.

"Turn around," Steffen ordered.

Amadeo took his sweet time, arrogantly displaying every angle of his carved physique as he did so. Steffen spanked the rounded ass to hurry him up, knowing this would only slow him down. Amadeo held onto the rails of the pool steps, the water coming to barely lap at his swaying ball sac. Spreading his feet on the steps, he gyrated like a pole dancer. The panoramic view of Palm Springs, with Last Chance off to one side, spread out beneath them, a city of tiny lights. Tiny auto horns in the far distance sounded like toys. More immediate was the rustling of royal palm fronds and the lowing of a nearby cattle herd, and sometimes the scent of cowhide wafted to them. But hey, they were ranchers. And being ranchers had built this prime example of architecture where Steffen could imagine spending the rest of his years.

"Take me," Amadeo said again, looking coquettishly over his shoulder. He wagged his ass, as though Steffen needed any more temptation. "Fill me with that big dick of yours."

A handy bottle of suntan oil greased up Steffen's cock. He didn't dare fist his own meat too ardently, though. He poured a palmful of oil and rubbed it into Amadeo's puckered anus. He covered the other man's back with his torso, murmuring, "I'm going to impale you on my dick, Amadeo. How do you like that?" He rubbed his cockhead against the entrance until he had to gasp and stop.

"I never knew the quarterback like to pound other boys up the ass. You have so many girls. Why do you want to hump another boy?"

"Because," Steffen grunted, breaching the tight ring and burrowing his cock deeper in his lover. "Other boys are bigger, meatier. They understand what real fucking is."

"Oh, *goddddd*, yeah! Fuck me, you big athletic dickhead!"

Steffen could practically feel the immense shudder that ran down Amadeo's spine as he was penetrated. He had to slap the curvy ass several more times just to distract himself, to stop himself from coming immediately. "Stand still, you fucking stoner," he snarled, playing the high school game. "I'm gonna violate you and ream you from top to bottom. You won't even know what happened."

"Fuck me, you nasty jock." Amadeo obscenely swiveled his hips, fucking the air. "Do me like you do all your girlfriends."

"You boys need a cheerleader? It appears you're doing just fine on your own, but maybe the stoner could use a pair of tits to suck on."

Abruptly the two men stopped moving, gasping in air.

Willow stood there on the terrace, wearing one of the low-cut minidresses she'd been favoring of late. Her arms crossed in front of her bosom only served as a shelf to lift and buoy up her tits, and Steffen gaped with desire.

Then he smiled. "Sure. Cheerleaders are always welcome."

* * * *

Willow squealed with delight. She was so excited she wheeled away from her home office desk, rolling in her chair until she hit the wall. "*Ahhhhh!*" Like a little girl she squirmed with happiness then panted for a minute until she could roll back to the desk and look at the computer screen again.

Yes. There she was. In her in-box. The Russian adoption agency had finally sent photos of her new daughter, Lavinia.

With pounding heart, Willow's hand reached for the mouse to click open the attachments. Things had been going well lately…too good to be true. She kept waiting for the other shoe to drop, for some disaster to befall them. She had even come to grips with her weight. She knew she'd never be slender again as she was when she smoked cigarettes, but the beauty of it was, *neither of her men seemed to mind.* Not her husband, not their lover. Neither had ever made a "fat" crack. She still tried to eat reasonably, but the weight just wouldn't melt off as it did in days of old.

There. Lavinia. She was perfect. Willow marveled at the photos for several more minutes before printing them to show the men. The girl was three years old and her only alleged health issue was asthma. She was probably malnutritioned, too, with several vitamin deficiencies. But now the three of them could fly to St. Petersburg and visit with Lavinia, after having heard so much about her.

Willow had to step out the sliding glass door of the office because she couldn't walk through the enormous, domed living room. The sparkling starry sky showed in the pie-like skylights cut into the roof and its eaves. She had seen this sky a hundred times before like this, but tonight it felt special. The butt plug inside of her swiveled about, sending delicious shivers into her innards. She knew that with a child they would have to start confining their play sessions to the locked bedroom.

But right now, her two men were going hard at it on the shallow end of the pool at the steps. Willow watched for awhile, admiring their form. She loved the part of being a *voyeuse* when she knew her husband and lover weren't watching her, and now she knew they hadn't spied her yet. She placed the photos safely on a terrace table and made sure to stay in the shadows, admiring the flexing of Steffen's ass muscles as he drilled his partner. It was always such a sight to behold, the rippling of the muscles in the two men's backs as they humped each other.

"Fuck me, you nasty jock," snarled Amadeo, and she knew they were playing the high school game. It was scintillating to think that after so many decades, the idol of Amadeo's youth was finally eagerly plunging his cock inside him to the hilt. Amadeo was getting what he had wanted so long ago, when he'd first ogled Steffen showering in that locker room.

Willow couldn't stop herself from stepping out from the shadows. "You boys need a cheerleader?"

Steffen gaped for a few seconds and then grinned, so Willow kicked off her heeled sandals to take a few steps down into the pool. Yanking down her bodice, she offered her tits to Amadeo. He eagerly sucked on them, sending thrills through her pussy. Steffen paused in his fucking to lean around Amadeo's shoulder and assist. Cupping her tit, he held it aloft for his lover to suck.

"There," Steffen said with satisfaction. "That's all you needed. We're always sucking on cheerleader's tits, but I guess you stoners don't get to often."

This increased Amadeo's hunger, and now he yanked the dress down over her shoulders so that both tits popped out, bouncing in the warm night air. Amadeo voraciously went from tit to tit, nibbling and suckling both. Willow poured a handful of the suntan oil to grease up Amadeo's erect penis, causing him to gasp. His eyes rolled into his head, and he tossed his head back as she stroked.

She murmured, "You loser stoners don't get much, do you? Haven't you ever had a cheerleader jack you off?"

"God, no," Amadeo groaned.

"Not so fast." Steffen removed her hand from Amadeo's prick. "Willow. You got your plug in? Give him your ass."

"Ooh." Willow liked that idea. They had been allowing Amadeo to butt fuck her for several months now. It was a good solution to the problem of Steffen's jealousy and Steffen's idea that there was still a slight chance she might get pregnant. If she ever did, by some miracle, he wanted to know that *he* was the father. And Amadeo's cock didn't have the girth of Steffen's. Wearing the butt plug had stretched her to the point where there was now no element of pain to it—merely the pleasurable aspects.

"Turn around, Miss Cheerleader."

Willow allowed Steffen to boss her like that. Now she was submitting to two men at once, and she felt desired, wanted. She turned, lifting her skirt, allowing Amadeo to remove the plug.

Amadeo murmured, "You're all stretched out for me. We both like playing the ponies, don't we, Steffen?"

"God, yes," groaned Steffen. "Oil up that asshole, you fucking stoner. You know you want to fuck her."

Clinging to the pool rails, Willow squirmed, shimmying her shoulders and wiggling her butt the way she knew Amadeo liked. "That's it," she encouraged when he tickled her asshole with the oil. "Fill me up with your long dick, Amadeo. I want to feel it plowing me, spurting inside me, coming—*ah!*"

Willow hadn't expected Amadeo to enter her so swiftly! It felt as though all the air was sucked from her lungs, it was so sudden. She felt his penis shudder inside her, and his deep groans vibrated through her pussy and abdomen. She recovered quickly as the three of them started to move in tandem. She loved the way she could feel Steffen screwing Amadeo as Amadeo screwed her. Every time Steffen speared his lover up the ass, Amadeo's cock would twitch deep inside of her. Amadeo was being assaulted from both sides.

"You know how to push me over the edge, Amadeo," she said over her shoulder. "You like to be pushed to your limits, but you know how to push me, too."

"Oh, yeah?" Amadeo growled with pride, but clearly didn't know exactly what she referred to.

"I'm accepting your big dick from behind," she breathed, "and I need you to spank me."

Amadeo caught on rapidly. He slapped her ass a few times, but when she straightened up her torso, he moved to swatting her pussy.

Yes. "That's it," she purred, spreading her feet wider on the step. Every time Amadeo slapped her clit, it sent a warmth radiating through her torso. He slapped her just hard enough to sting and bring blood rushing to engorge her clit, pulping up her pussy lips, making a dull mushy sound when he spanked her. She found herself moaning and undulating her spine as Amadeo fucked her.

That encouraged him, too. "You've been a bad, slutty cheerleader, haven't you?" he snarled as he expertly held her ass up with the strength of his hips. Willow could feel Steffen pausing too, on the verge of climax no doubt, his penis buried deep inside his lover.

"Oh, yes," Willow agreed, in a slutty tone. "I've been very, very bad."

"Then spank her!" Steffen suddenly urged in a higher tone than normal, and Willow knew Steffen couldn't hold back anymore.

Amadeo's pussy slaps rang out over the terrace as he ground his cock inside Willow. "I'm going to come," she had to warn him, so he wouldn't stop as his own orgasm overtook him.

He slapped and rubbed her professionally now, and her orgasmic waves clenched her uterus and her anus as it clutched at Amadeo's ejaculating cock. She made only muted choking sounds as her orgasm continued, seizing up every organ and making her whimper with ecstasy. "Come, come," she was finally able to whisper, as though the men needed her encouragement. Amadeo's cock absolutely gushed inside her, depositing such a load she could already feel it trickling down her inner thighs. Steffen drilled him from the other side, pounding him mercilessly with his spurting cock.

Steffen was the first to withdraw, exhaling hugely. He backstroked out across the illuminated pool while the other couple remained locked together. Steffen splashed and groaned loudly as he apparently did some underwater somersaults, then kicked and crawled some more back to their end of the pool. Amadeo's cock was still twitching inside Willow when he reached them. He slapped Amadeo on the shoulder.

"Can't get enough? Listen, I've got an early start tomorrow morning at work, so I'm going to fire up the grill now, do some steaks and fish, call it an early night."

"Good idea," said Amadeo, suddenly the picture of the happy cattleman, pulling out of Willow and splashing water on his cock.

"There's some salad from last night. The lettuce might be a little wilted, but it's still all right. I didn't put dressing on it yet."

Willow's pussy still burned with the spanking she'd received, and semen seeped down her calves now, but she hauled herself out of the pool by the rails. "Yeah, I have to get back to the Searchlight right now. The temporary chef at the Cavern isn't familiar enough with the recipes. Guys, first, there's something I want to show you. I just got an e-mail—"

"Who the fuck's at the front door?" Steffen manfully dragged himself out of the pool without using the steps, vaulting over the edge and pulling himself up.

"I'm not expecting anyone," Willow said, stepping back into her sandals. She used a towel hanging over an outdoor chair to towel off the semen, careful not to drip on the photos of Lavinia. Amadeo vanished, using the sliding glass door to enter the master bedroom and, presumably, bath. Willow wandered around the terrace. She had fired her Cavern on the Green chef last month because she was too exacting, as Steffen said. She had cooked for Matt for many years and thought she knew a thing or two, and she had just lost it one night when the old chef had used inferior tripe in the pepper pot soup. Now she regretted having been so rash. She didn't need any additional duties, especially with a trip to St. Petersburg coming up. Amadeo thought she should apologize to the old chef and bring him back, but she felt too foolish.

"What a splendid evening to go for a swim!"

The perpetually cheerful Carl Bogart was suddenly on the terrace, accompanied by a very chipper and gorgeous blonde gal. The girl had luscious features—that was the only word to describe her. Exotic and luscious. Her hair was so frothy and whipped it made Willow hungry for a creamy dessert. "Hi, Carl. You didn't need to come here. I was about to head on down to the motel anyway, help out in the kitchen."

Carl, having quit Chas White's employ, was now her motel manager. "That would defeat the entire purpose, Miss Paige!" He still insisted on calling her Miss Paige. “I wanted to introduce you to Rose here.” He displayed the women standing next to him. Her slight overbite gave her an adorable, ducky look, and Willow liked her instantly.

“Hi, Rose.” She shook hands. Why was Carl showing off yet one more in his stable of pretty fillies? Being a motel manager apparently had its perks, because Carl was never alone.

“Nice to meet you, Willow. I’ve been down to your motel and the Cavern. I like the menu you have framed on the wall but I don’t think I’d try to cook anything from it.”

Willow laughed. It was so unexpected that Rose meant the framed Sunset Palomino Ranch “menu” she had hung in the lobby, she burst out in laughter. “No, don’t ever try to cook anything from *that* menu!”

Carl glared at the women with irritation. “That’s not why we came here, Miss Paige. Here, maybe your husband can explain.”

Carl gestured at Amadeo, who was rounding the terrace from the master bedroom side of the house. Clad now decently in khaki slacks and a new Hawaiian shirt, he smoothed his thick black hair back from his forehead and came forward politely.

“Oh. Rose, is it? Right. Willow, Carl showed me Rose’s resumé earlier. Quite impressive.”

Willow was confused. “So you’ve met my husband?”

“Yes. Earlier at the motel. I dropped off my resumé. And I presume this is your other partner?”

Willow was already experienced in how oddly people could react to their arrangement. They had decided she would wed Amadeo. He would want their progeny to inherit his ranch, and it would give her a good backup plan if her motel failed. So nominally, Amadeo was the “husband” and Steffen was the “partner.” Even if gay marriage *were* allowed in California at the moment, their arrangement would still defy all attempts to categorize it legally, but it worked.

“Yes, this is Steffen Werner. You’re a chef, then?”

Rose talked a bit about her cooking experience, and she sounded like she might be a good fit. They made plans to meet at the Cavern restaurant at the Searchlight in an hour or so, and the couple departed, but not without Rose casting a meaningful look at the butt plug that still sat next to the pool steps.

"I think we'll get along great," Willow assured her.

Amadeo had been rummaging around barbecuing slabs of beef and a halibut steak for Steffen, but Willow hadn't shown them the photos of their future daughter yet. She sidled up to Steffen, who was being the manly mixologist at the wet bar. She said nothing, just held one of the photos in front of his face. His eyes flickered back and forth several times, unsure what he was seeing. He looked at the glass with the ice cubes, then back to the photo.

Willow knew the moment it dawned on Steffen what he looked at. The ice tongs clattered onto the bar as he slowly wiped off his hands on a rag without taking his eyes from the photo. As though in slow motion, he reached out for the picture.

"Yup," Willow agreed with his unspoken remarks. "That's Lavinia, all right. We can fly to St. Petersburg on the twelfth to visit with her and fill out more paperwork."

"Holy…" Steffen took a few zombie-like steps until he was directly underneath one of the overhead cans of light. "Lavinia. I can't believe it. She's beautiful, Willow."

"What?" yelled Amadeo, dropping his meat fork onto the grill. In a flash he was at Steffen's side, practically elbowing the other man aside to see the photo. "Oh my God."

"I have more pictures." Willow gave a few to Amadeo and he grabbed them greedily.

Steffen's eyes shined as he looked up from his picture. "We're really doing this. We're finally going to have a child."

Amadeo scoffed. "Say 'finally' about yourself, old man. I'm two years younger than you *and* a cattle magnate. I can have children when I'm eighty."

"Sure you can," Willow assured him. They stood in a tight little circle breathing on the photos. It all felt so momentous, a minute in time that would never be repeated, looking at the first photos of their first child. Willow was certain she would blow the moment by saying something goofy and ridiculous. "But I'll be seventy-four by then, so I think I'll be done with kids."

"Right," agreed Steffen, kissing her forehead. "By then you'll have moved onto our great-grandkids."

Nothing had ever felt this right. Willow had always blundered her way through life, hoping that things turned out okay in the end, or at least that no one was mortally wounded as she stumbled along. She had always just held her breath and hoped for the best. With Steffen and Amadeo, for the first time ever she had certainty. She didn't have to lie awake at night staring at the ceiling, a sense of doom and unease looming over her.

For the first time in her life, it all seemed *real* to Willow. Her future with her two men was tangible. She could reach out and touch it. The two men were her stability, her home, her rock. They would still be there in the morning. And for that, she was grateful.

THE END

WWW.KARENMERCURYAUTHOR.BLOGSPOT.COM

ABOUT THE AUTHOR

Karen's first three novels were historical fiction involving pre-colonial African explorers. Since she was always either accused or praised (depending on how you look at it) for writing overly steamy sex scenes, erotic romance was the natural next step. She lives near Napa, California, where she shoots archery, collects minerals, plays with her little Newfoundland pup Myshkin, and does other "guy" things.

For all titles by Karen Mercury, please visit
www.bookstrand.com/karen-mercury

Siren Publishing, Inc.
www.SirenPublishing.com

CPSIA information can be obtained at www.ICGtesting.com
Printed in the USA
LVOW07s1401080614

389114LV00018B/1132/P

9 781627 404136